The Mosaic Woman

RESA NELSON

a local Salem author!!

Copyright © 2021 Resa Nelson

Cover art © 2021 Eric Wilder

All rights reserved.

First Edition May 2021. This book is a work of fiction. Names, characters, places and incidents are the invention of the author, and any resemblance to any actual persons, living or dead, event, or locale is entirely coincidental. The unauthorized reproduction or distribution of this or any copyrighted work is illegal.

ISBN: 9798734523445

ACKNOWLEDGEMENTS

Many thanks to my fellow authors, Carla Johnson and Tom Sweeney, who read this novel before publication and gave me excellent feedback.

THE MOSAIC WOMAN

CHAPTER 1

Descending from the sky to the island city of VainGlory in the arms of a drone taxi, Zuri's grin shifted into a grimace when her feet touched ground and the drone released her.

She adjusted her Slim Goggles, which wrapped around her head and across her eyes like sunglasses. They projected a small screen in front of her face, currently showing the retreating image of the drone taxi that had carried her in its rollercoaster harness for a short distance across the sea to this island, depositing her on a bullseye painted on the harbor.

Beyond the dock where she now stood, streetlamps arched high above a maze of sidewalks winding through a myriad of fountains and greenery.

One of the streetlamps turned as if

looking at Zuri, and its recessed bulb turned on and cast its light in her direction.

A moment of panic paralyzed Zuri.

This is real. It's truly happening.

For the past ten years, all Zuri had wanted was fame, and VainGlory provided the fastest path to that goal. Fame meant happiness, something Zuri longed to find.

But in this moment, Zuri felt the truth unfolding around her. Accepting the invitation to VainGlory required giving up all she'd ever known.

The streetlamp swung its beam at the surrounding peers. Those other streetlamps followed their companion's beam when it pointed back at Zuri. A heavy hum reverberated from them.

Here, everything would be foreign and new. She'd be starting from the bottom, trying to navigate the hazards of making her way back to the top where she belonged.

Zuri made an attempt to calm her nerves.

I'm not losing everything. Just my earthy surroundings and route. The other things will stay the same.

"Zuri?"

She checked the display in front of her face at the sound of a woman's voice, but Zuri saw no one.

"That model doesn't work here. You can see things, but you can't see people. I won't show up. You have to remove your goggles."

Zuri's body trembled at the awful suggestion. Her panic escalated into terror. When Zuri spoke, her voice shook so hard that she didn't recognize it. "Take them off? What if I don't want to?"

The invisible woman's voice took a sharp tone. "You can't enter VainGlory unless you do what I say. I'm your supervisor. Donna." The woman paused. "If you don't want to be supervised, it's a one-way ticket back to where you came from."

Zuri thought she might not be ready for VainGlory yet. If she left, maybe she could come back another time. Maybe sometime next year. That would give her time to build up her courage.

"If you leave," Donna said, "you won't be invited back. That means you'll never achieve more than what you've already accomplished."

For the past ten years, Zuri had strived toward the goal of arriving in VainGlory and making her way to the top. Ten long years. If she gave up now, she'd never get anywhere. All the years she'd worked so hard would be for nothing.

And it wouldn't be only Zuri's dream that would die.

"All right," Zuri said. She steeled her willpower with encouraging thoughts.

Make it quick, like ripping off a bandage. You can do this.

Zuri took off her Slim Goggles with a swift hand, folded them, and stuffed them in the satchel of essentials she'd brought. The harshness of daylight made her flinch.

But Zuri sensed more than daylight. Dozens of streetlamps directed beams of light at her.

Donna spun away from Zuri to face them. "Knock it off! She's invited. She's approved."

The beams dimmed and then went dark. The streetlamps turned back to their previous positions, no longer seeming to stare at Zuri.

Donna turned back to face her.

A wretched discomfort forced Zuri to look down at her feet, unable to bear the opportunity to look into the eyes of her new supervisor.

"Good," Donna said, nodding her approval at seeing Zuri no longer wearing her Slim Goggles. "That sense of shock you're feeling right now is something everyone goes through when they come to VainGlory for the first time. It's normal."

Zuri intended to speak in a strong and confident tone, surprised to hear herself mumble. "It is?"

Zuri heard slow footsteps coming toward her. Frightened at the sound, she took a stumbling step back, keeping her gaze on the ground.

The footsteps halted. "It's very normal.

But everything I'm asking you to do this morning is necessary. It's how you transition. It's unnerving. Everyone says it feels unnatural. But it's necessary."

Zuri tried to speak, but she mumbled again, this time saying no words that even she could recognize.

"Ultimately," Donna said, "you're the one who will benefit. If you do as I say, I can get you off to a strong start as early as today. But first you need to look at me."

Do it quick.

Zuri clung to her satchel as if it had the power to protect her from lions. Then she looked up at Donna, who wore no goggles at all. Dressed in slim black pants, a simple white shirt, and a black coat with a dozen pewter button closures, she conjured the sensibility of a military officer. The woman's eyes appeared dark and stern, and they gazed with too much intensity at Zuri.

Unnerved, Zuri used a trick she'd learned long ago. She shifted her own gaze to land on Donna's throat. That way, Zuri could avoid her supervisor's eyes while appearing to look directly at her face.

"Good." Donna pointed at slim poles around them that stretched skyward. "That is why your goggles don't work. The city has a privacy wall."

"I don't see a wall."

"That's what we call it. It's more of an invisible shield that blocks unauthorized transmissions from coming in and going out. For example, have you seen much of VainGlory before coming here?"

Zuri considered the question. She'd seen plenty of the people who lived here but little of the city itself. "No."

"That's why. Because of the privacy wall. Your goggles are unauthorized. We'll provide a replacement. One that's authorized." Donna spread her arms wide. "Welcome to VainGlory. Where fame is the name of the game."

Relieved at the unspoken invitation to look away from Donna, Zuri started at the sight that had been right in front of her all this time.

At the edge of the bullseye where Zuri had landed stood a marble walkway surrounded by canals filled with clean azure water, stretching far ahead and to either side. As if on cue, dozens of fountains erupted alongside the canals.

"Walk with me," Donna said. "I'll give you a basic tour. When we're done, you need to make a decision, so pay attention." She turned her back on Zuri and walked forward.

Zuri hurried to catch up and walk alongside her new supervisor, while keeping her attention on their surroundings. As long as she didn't have to look at anyone, Zuri could carry on a conversation.

Streetlamps lining the marble walkway

turned to aim at Zuri. In unison, they beamed streams of yellow light at her. The streetlamps hummed angrily.

Zuri and her supervisor faltered to a halt.

"Stop that!" Donna shouted at the streetlamps. "I already told you she's supposed to be here."

When they failed to respond, she flattened one hand and swiped it against the air in front of her. "The city isn't recognizing a new recruit because she has just arrived. She hasn't been to the Welcome Center yet. Take care of it."

Moments later, the streetlamps shuddered. The yellow beams of light died out, and the streetlamps turned away from Zuri as if in shame.

Catching a glimpse, Zuri noticed camera lenses mounted on top of each light.

"That's more like it," Donna muttered. "The city didn't recognize you. All it had to go on was your identity chip. The city thought you were an unauthorized intruder. Safety is a top priority in VainGlory. Our citizens count on it. Most people leave their doors unlocked and the keys to their boats in the ignition. That's how safe the city is."

Zuri couldn't help but rub the fleshy web between her thumb and forefinger where her identity chip had been implanted when she reached the legal age of 12. Like everyone else, she rarely thought about it.

As they continued walking, Donna gestured toward the fountains and maze of canals. "This is the water garden. It surrounds the city. A perimeter, of sorts." She held up a warning hand. "And before you ask, the city has plenty of options for getting around, from drone taxis to fast-tracks. Of course, most residents rarely leave home, because they don't have to. We are walking by choice. I want you to take in what you see. Drink it in. You'll need to remember it."

Normally, Zuri would have blanched at the suggestion of walking. But she understood Donna's intent. The water garden filled Zuri with wonder and delight. The water from the canals smelled as fresh as summer rain. The fountains danced a dizzying array of movements, intricate and surprising.

As they walked, the canal alongside them widened. Several dolphins leapt out of it, twisting and turning in the air. Zuri cried out in surprise when a whale leapt into the wake the dolphins left behind. She darted a few steps ahead to avoid getting splashed.

Where the water garden ended, a more conventional garden began. Walking in silence, Zuri drank in the ever-changing scents of sweet flowers and freshly-mown grass. Slender trees delineated the boundaries, and their leaves rustled in the gentle wind. Like colorful spokes of a wheel, a group of long and triangular flower beds brimmed with crimson tulips, sunshine daffodils, and purple snapdragons.

"It's so perfect," Zuri said. "I've never seen anything like it."

"This is the Animated Garden. It's all engineered." Donna called out to the garden, "Tulips! Come to attention!"

Like soldiers, all the crimson tulips straightened their stems and petals so that they looked perfectly uniform.

Stunned, Zuri said, "Are they real flowers?"

"In a manner of speaking. Just don't try to pick any of them." Donna stopped and leaned down to pick up a small stone from the marble gravel lining the pathway. She tossed it toward a snapdragon, whose blossoms bared sparkling dagger-like teeth and lunged toward the pebble as it sailed past them.

Zuri jumped in surprise.

"It's a mechanism built in by the jewelers," Donna said. "The snaps have diamond teeth. The peonies and chrysanthemums have rubies and emeralds at their centers. They're meant to provide beauty to all. Theft is frowned upon. And usually prevented."

Although Zuri wanted to pepper Donna with questions, she remembered her supervisor's advice.

Everything I'm asking you to do this

morning is necessary. When we're done, you need to make a decision, so pay attention.

Trellises supporting ivy and white blossoms walked upright through the animated park, pausing when they encountered each other to band together and form geometric shapes. Large bumblebees and hummingbirds flitted through the air. One bird with a flashing red throat approached Zuri and hovered in front of her face.

"She's with me," Donna said to the hummingbird. "Be on your way."

Taking a closer look at the bird, Zuri noticed its metallic feathers before it zipped away with a rustling noise. "It's a robot."

Donna nodded. "The bees, too." She pointed ahead. "You might have noticed that the gardens are laid out like the outer rings of a target with the city as its center. The next ring is the Carnival of Animals."

Following Donna's pointing finger, Zuri caught her breath in wonder. Where the animated garden ended, lush green lawns began. A safari park revealed an array of transparent animals that roamed and appeared to graze on the grass.

"They're made of crystal," Donna said.

The animals glistened in the sunlight, and Zuri spotted no more than one of each. An elephant rubbed up against a tree, which cracked under its life-size height and weight. A tiger stalked through a stretch of tall, waving grass while eyeing an antelope that appeared to drink from a quartz pond. A koala snuggled among the branches of a tall tree. Encased in a large glass cube edged with frost, a polar bear stretched across a mound of snow.

A sudden movement caught Zuri's attention, and her jaw dropped in astonishment. "Is that a unicorn?"

A single-horned horse pawed the ground on top of a slight rise.

"It is," Donna said. "There's also a Pegasus, a centaur, and a dragon. I hear there's a gargoyle due to arrive next week." She pointed above the unicorn. "They prefer their space, but that bridge allows you to walk among them."

Zuri stared into the blank air above the unicorn until the outline of a bridge shimmered into view. "Is it made of crystal, too?"

"Partly. When people walk across it, they look like they're floating on air."

Zuri choked back tears of joy. All her life, she'd heard rumors of VainGlory, but she never dared believe them because images of the city were considered contraband. The few she'd seen showed little more than faces of its famous residents. What she'd seen since her arrival proved to be far more wondrous than anything she'd ever imagined.

A woman's petrified scream pierced the silence.

Zuri looked all around but saw no one. "Who was that?"

The unicorn whinnied in dismay.

Thrashing sounds churned from the large canal a short distance away in the water garden through which they had walked.

Zuri turned back to look. Dolphins leapt high in the air like salmon swimming upstream. A creature twice their size vaulted out of the water and snatched one dolphin in its jaws, crammed with rows of sharp teeth. Blood sprayed in a fountain from the shrieking dolphin's body before it disappeared under water with its attacker.

Zuri's heart raced. "What was that? What's happening?"

Donna spoke in a nonchalant tone. "Just a glitch. They happen from time to time. Nothing to be concerned about."

A small domed building of polished granite loomed ahead, and Donna led Zuri to its entrance. An engraved brass plate next to the door read "Welcome, New Residents."

Even when Donna spoke, Zuri kept her focus on the building.

"This is where we part ways. Inside, they'll fit you with a Personal Bubble and a DPA."

"DPA?"

"Digital Personal Assistant. From now on, our contact will be strictly through your

Bubble."

Despite Zuri's success in avoiding looking at her new supervisor's face, their conversation had been the longest in-person interaction Zuri had experienced during the past ten years. It exhausted her. Knowing she wouldn't have to go through this again gave her relief.

"Once they get you sorted out," Donna continued, "I'll take you to your new home and tell you about your first assignment."

Zuri walked into the Welcome Center, filled with the desperation of having been disconnected from her Slim Goggles for such a long time. Her hands trembled, and her throat felt dry. She clung to her satchel as if it were a security blanket, knowing her goggles rested safely inside should that desperation get the best of her.

Soon, Zuri told herself. *It won't be long until you're connected to the world again, and then everything will be alright.*

* * *

Donna watched Zuri walk into the Welcome Center until the door shut behind the young woman. "I need to speak to Franklin Buckingham," Donna said.

Like the movers and shakers of Vain-Glory, she rejected most kinds of direct connection to the world, whether the outside world or the insular world of this city.

Her one concession was calls.

Her earpiece buzzed moments later. Answering with a flick of her head, she said, "Donna here."

Silence weighed on the other end for a brief moment. Then a familiar male voice spoke. "She's here?"

"She's here."

"Any problems?"

"Nothing of significance. A scream. Probably someone creating something for the Murder Channel. Then one of the sharks got loose."

Silence weighed heavier. "How did she respond?"

"Like you'd expect. But when I sent her to the Welcome Center, she forgot what she'd just seen and heard. You know how they are."

Franklin Buckingham sighed with relief on the other end of the call. "They get used to constant interruptions. It's normal for them."

Donna smiled. "So is forgetting. If you want to make them forget, all you have to do is interrupt and point them in a new direction." Knowing her place and her responsibility to Franklin Buckingham, she said, "How soon do you need her?"

"That's unclear at the moment. Possibly as early as next week. Or it could be sometime in the next few months. I won't know until the tests are done."

"Understood. I'll make sure she's ready when you are." The click in her ear let Donna know he'd hung up.

She dreaded the necessity of monitoring the new girl for the next few days or weeks or however long it took. Donna took little joy in knowing she had ways to do so without resorting to the use of a Bubble or other noxious device.

But what had to be done had to be done.

More thrashing sounds erupted from the distant water garden.

Donna made a mental note to have a discussion with Maintenance as she walked past the Welcome Center and headed toward her home office.

Damn sharks.

CHAPTER 2

Zuri delighted in the fact that her life so far had been marked by constant advances in technology.

Here she stood in a pristine white room at the threshold of a pristine city. As directed by the technician wearing a white lab coat, Zuri sat in a padded chair that reclined, raising her feet on the attached rest. Lights glared overhead.

She balked when told to relinquish her Slim Goggles. With reluctance, she took her time digging them out of her satchel. Zuri tried to cling to them when the technician pried them out of her fingers. "I need them. They're prescription."

The technician laughed and said, "Forget prescription. The Personal Bubble automatically senses your vision and corrects it." The technician tossed the Slim Goggles into a large cylinder marked "trash," opened a cabinet by the wall, and brought forth a small transparent box that appeared to be empty. Opening the box and holding it in front of Zuri, the technician said, "If you wore contacts before Slim Goggles were invented, you should remember how to put them in."

"I remember contacts," Zuri said. "But you said my Personal Bubble will fix my vision."

The technician smiled. "Think of these as your gateway to your Personal Bubble. You can't get there without them."

With a tentative hand, Zuri removed what appeared to be old-fashioned contact lenses and popped them in her eyes.

The world as she knew it changed forever.

At first, Zuri found herself inside a white bubble the size of a small room. While she could sense the Welcome Center examination room outside the round bubble walls, the reality of it was masked by a pale opaqueness. The technician's voice sounded distant and muffled. Every movement made the technician look like a shadow outside a window on a rainy day. Zuri couldn't remember the color of the exam room's walls or what type of floor it had. From inside her Personal Bubble, the room looked dark and murky.

"Testing," the technician said in a voice

that boomed loud and clear. "Can you hear me, Zuri?"

She turned in place, seeing nothing but the round white wall of her Bubble. "Yes," Zuri said. "I can hear you."

"Good," the technician said. "You might want to brace yourself for this next part."

Before Zuri could ask why, her white Bubble wall filled with thousands of curved images, like tiles on a bathroom wall. Images of people, art, war, buildings, animals, and landscapes. Images of horror and beauty. Images of peace and terror. A cacophony of sounds reverberated through the Bubble, echoing in all directions until Zuri couldn't tell up from down or right from left.

Dazed and frightened, she shouted, "Make it stop!"

"Hold on, Zuri," the technician said. "We're almost there."

Zuri clapped her hands over her face to shut out the attack of sight and sound, willing it to leave her alone without success.

Moments later, as promised, silence.

Tentatively, Zuri let her trembling hands drift away from her face.

The Bubble wall stood white and empty again, except for a cartoon figure of a bundle of wires that spoke with the technician's voice. "Better?"

The bundle of wires shaped itself into a stick figure.

"I don't understand," Zuri said. "Where

am I?"

The stick figure put its hands on its hips. "Welcome to your Personal Bubble." It waved one hand, and the white wall surrounding her filled with colorful and animated icons. "Navigation is simple. All you have to do is bring your focus to whichever place you want to go. Try it."

Speechless at the symphony of sight and sound that filled her vision, Zuri scanned the icons until she recognized Book of Friends. "That one," she said, pointing at it.

The Book of Friends icon—an open book filled with short videos of everyone she knew—enlarged until it stood like an open doorway in front of her. All of the other icons remained visible in the background but became muted in color and sound. As usual, the videos of her friends chattered and waved.

"What do I do when I'm done with it? When I want to go somewhere else?"

The stick figure swept a wiry arm across the hundreds of icons covering the bubble wall behind the dominant Book of Friends. "Just shift your focus."

Zuri scanned the smaller icons until she recognized another place where she liked to spend time. She pointed at it. "That one."

The Book of Friends doorway minimized back to icon size and slipped back in place among the others while the SeeMe icon—a jigsaw puzzle of images captured across the world of tourist sites, food, and parties—came forward and commanded Zuri's attention. The images began rotating on a carousel, and the people inside those images called out to her. "See me!" a little girl walking on the Great Wall of China shouted. A fork next to a fancy chocolate dessert on a porcelain plate bounced up and waved while screaming, "Ignore her—see me!"

Unable to resist temptation, Zuri reached out with an empty hand until she realized she didn't know how to interact with them. "How do I show my approval?"

"Your PDA will show you." A cable port materialized alongside the SeeMe doorway that burst with rotating and boisterous photos. The stick figure unfurled until it looked like a strand of cooked spaghetti, plugged into the port, and disappeared through it.

The port then morphed into the image of a human-like silver robot with amber eyes that glowed like traffic lights. The glowing eyes turned and fixated on Zuri. "I will be your Personal Digital Assistant, Miss. You may call me Benjamin. How may I be of service?"

Zuri had never encountered anything like Benjamin before. For the past ten years, her connection to the world had been simplistic and intuitive. She'd never needed any kind of assistance before, and she did not like the idea of being dependent on anyone or anything.

On the other hand, the Personal Bubble brought her world to life in breath-taking detail. Already, Zuri felt more connected to all the places she loved than she'd ever experienced before.

Maybe having a Personal Digital Assistant wasn't such a bad thing. Surely, everyone who lived in VainGlory had a PDA. The Personal Bubble was a luxury unlike anything Zuri had known until now, and the PDA appeared to be part of that luxury.

She answered Benjamin's question by pointing at the SeeMe doorway. "How do I stop the revolution? How do I approve?"

"With a simple pointing gesture," Benjamin said. His amber eyes darkened for a moment. He demonstrated. "Point at the frame to start and stop the rotation." The carousel responded to his pointing metallic finger and halted before the photos Zuri liked disappeared out of rotation. "Then point at whichever image you want for approval. If you disapprove, punch at it with your fist."

Following instructions, Zuri pointed at the little girl on the Great Wall and the chocolate dessert. A red stamp reading "Approved by Zuri" hovered over each photo before sinking into its corner.

The sudden sound of sweeping violins and gentle bassoons made Zuri jump.

"Nothing to fear, Miss," Benjamin said. "What you now hear is nothing but your Personal Soundtrack."

Zuri felt her jaw go slack with confusion. "Soundtrack? What soundtrack?"

Benjamin wrung his metallic hands and took a small step forward. "The soundtrack to your life, of course."

Zuri paused and listened as the tune lightened and brightened.

The voice of a girl sang

Happy and calm
That's what I am.
Happy and calm as a clam.
Yes, I am.

Raising her voice to be heard over the song, Zuri said, "I thought the most famous singers and musicians lived in VainGlory. This isn't one of them."

"That is correct," Benjamin said. "Your Soundtrack plays mostly in the background, especially when you're visiting these places. It guides your feelings." Once again, he swept his arm toward the hundreds of icons surrounding her like a dome. "But the Soundtrack takes center stage whenever your attention is required by someone in VainGlory. In this case, your supervisor is calling."

In that moment, Zuri realized this morning's face-to-face encounter had left her feeling traumatized. She couldn't bear anything like it again so soon. Her throat clenched, and her heartrate raced with anxiety while the girl sang again.

*Happy and calm
That's what I am.*

"This song is supposed to tell me how to feel?" Zuri said. "What if I don't want to feel happy and calm?"

"But you do feel happy and calm, Miss. You must. After all, you've arrived in Vain-Glory for the first time this morning, and now your supervisor has a very exciting assignment for you. Why wouldn't you feel happy and calm?"

The silver robot hurried to stand in front of the SeeMe doorway. With the flick of one shining hand, he dismissed it back to its small icon status on the bubble wall behind him. "Incoming message from your supervisor, Miss."

Zuri averted her gaze from the bubble wall surrounding her and stared at her feet instead.

Donna's voice boomed throughout the bubble, as if echoing inside a cave. "How do you like your Personal Bubble?"

Zuri tried to speak loud and clear, but her voice came out as a whisper. "It's great."

"Please, Miss," Benjamin whispered

next to her ear. "There's nothing to fear. You're quite safe. I'm in control of how people appear here. If you don't like what I've chosen, simply notify me, and I'll be more than happy to change it."

Zuri didn't know if she should trust her PDA, but the thought that he controlled how Donna appeared inside Zuri's Personal Bubble intrigued her. Zuri looked up before she could think twice.

A cartoonish pink caterpillar inched across the space in front of Zuri where the icons had become doorways. It reminded her of bubble gum.

The caterpillar halted and sat up on its haunches. "Is anything wrong?" the caterpillar said in Donna's voice.

Zuri sagged with relief. The experience of meeting and being so physically close to her new supervisor had been unnerving, but talking to cartoons was easy. "Everything is fine."

"Good." The caterpillar gave an approving nod. Its tiny black legs wiggled while it remained on its haunches. "I have your first assignment. Tonight is your launch."

"Tonight?" Zuri said in alarm. "But I just got here. Can't you reschedule me? I'm not ready."

The caterpillar waivered and tumbled onto its back. Its legs wiggled in the air. "There's plenty of time to get ready. Choose one thing, and that will be the launch."

Desperation tightened Zuri's throat. She'd assumed she'd have weeks to prepare. Launching tonight would be impossible.

What have I gotten myself into? What if I'm not good enough?

Before Zuri could protest again, the caterpillar righted itself and inched until its back rounded as if it were a frightened cat. "Remember what I told you earlier about taking note of the tour I gave you. Select one location. That's where your launch will happen."

Zuri's mind raced, filled with memories of all she'd seen earlier this morning. Then an alarming thought occurred to her. "What about the privacy wall? How can I launch if the privacy wall keeps the rest of the world out?"

The caterpillar crawled forward until its back flattened. "Think about what you've seen inside your bubble so far. Has any place you normally visit been blocked?"

"No," Zuri said, now confused. "But I haven't posted anything of my own. Or contacted anyone outside VainGlory."

"You can do that," the caterpillar said. "The privacy wall blocks any images or words that shouldn't leave the city. It's automatic. When you launch, everyone in VainGlory will see everything, including the location you choose and how you use it—that's the purpose of the launch. If you choose wisely, you'll be a viral success. Anyone outside VainGlory will see only what you launch and none of the surroundings."

"I see." A sudden pang of guilt gnawed at Zuri. From the moment she'd first set foot inside VainGlory, the excitement had dazed her to the point where she'd forgotten the one thing she'd promised. "I need to talk to you about my business partner. She's like a sister to me, and I wouldn't be here without her."

The cartoon caterpillar froze for a moment and then flickered. It turned toward Benjamin, standing far behind it, and said, "Assistant, interpret."

Zuri's stomach churned. Had she made a misstep? Done something wrong? If so, what?

Surprisingly, the robot appeared to detect her discomfort. He waved a hand at the caterpillar, which froze in place. "Nothing to worry about, Miss. This isn't a live conversation. It's a recorded message. You may ask questions, but they must be made in a clear and precise way so that the recording can calculate how to answer." With another wave, he freed the caterpillar and addressed it. "Miss Zuri appears to have a question about another person."

The caterpillar rotated its head to gaze at Zuri again. "Proceed."

Zuri shuddered, unsure how to ask for

what she needed and afraid to fail. Words popped out of her mouth before she could think. "When you first contacted me about moving to VainGlory, I asked if my business partner, Mae Lin, could move here, too. She's the brains behind what we do. I don't know if I can do anything without her."

A fly buzzed in a circle around the caterpillar's head, and the insects stared at each other in contemplation.

Benjamin whispered, "She's parsing your question and searching the main database for an answer."

"Database?" Zuri said. "What database?"

"The one database that connects all information in VainGlory, of course."

The fly paused long enough for the caterpillar to rise up on its haunches and eat it.

The sound of chomping made Zuri's stomach queasy.

"Mae Lin," the caterpillar said. "Yes, she is your business partner. But there is no need for her to be in VainGlory."

Had their meeting been in person like this morning, Zuri would have mumbled her acquiescence but left riddled with guilt. Talking to a cartoonish caterpillar eased her apprehension about standing up to her new supervisor.

"I need her," Zuri said. "I work better when she's nearby."

In truth, while Zuri had worked with Mae Lin for most of the past ten years, they rarely saw each other in person. They spent a great deal of time together in the virtual world.

They'd met soon after Zuri began her career. Their success had been gradual but steady.

For as long as they'd known each other, Zuri and Mae Lin had planned on becoming famous. Convinced they were good enough for VainGlory, they'd planned their move together, never imagining that anyone would consider splitting up their team.

When Zuri received her invitation to VainGlory but Mae Lin was left empty-handed, Zuri agreed to pave the way for her friend. If they had to be split up, it wouldn't be for long.

Now that she was here in VainGlory without Mae Lin, doubts assailed Zuri. Could she even succeed without her friend?

And the thought of failure was unbearable. If Zuri failed, wouldn't it destroy the partnership with Mae Lin that they both cherished?

"You will be fine without her," the caterpillar said. "However, if you succeed tonight, you will advance. When you advance to the highest tower, it will be acceptable to invite your partner to VainGlory." The caterpillar waved its legs. "Remember: fame is the name of the game."

The caterpillar then winked out of existence.

"Wait!" Zuri shouted. "What happens tonight?"

Benjamin cleared his robotic throat. "I will be most happy to explain, Miss. Please follow me."

The robot turned his back to Zuri and walked through the domed wall of icons, still animated and crying out for Zuri's attention.

"Wait!" Zuri called out again. "What am I supposed to do?"

"Follow," Benjamin said, his voice now growing distant.

Zuri hesitated. She could hear Benjamin but no longer saw him. She saw nothing beyond the wall of icons, which filled her entire field of vision.

The idea of walking seemed precarious at best. But she decided to follow the sound of Benjamin's voice and hurried toward it.

Several running steps later, Zuri crashed headfirst into a wall.

"PDA," the technician's voice called out from nothingness. "Guide your client! She missed the door."

Benjamin poked his head through the wall of icons and stared at Zuri. His amber eyes flashed as if warning of an impending storm. "Apologies, Miss. But you must hurry. There's too much to be done and little time in which to accomplish it!"

CHAPTER 3

Hesitant at first to instruct the wall of icons to fade enough to detect the real world outside her Personal Bubble, Zuri accepted Benjamin's advice to do so. Satisfied that all of her favorite places were still visible and accessible, she glanced at the outlines of the buildings outside just enough to keep pace with her Personal Digital Assistant.

At the same time, she asked for his help in making a call beyond the shores of Vain-Glory, promising Benjamin that she'd pay enough attention to walking to keep from bumping into anything else.

Zuri gestured the TalkToMe icon to come forward and open its doorway, and then pressed the image of her friend. Soon, Mae Lin's smiling face filled the space.

"Zuri! Are you there? Is everything OK?" Mae Lin's smile faded. "All I see is your face. Everything around you is black. Are you in a dark room?"

Seeing her friend filled Zuri with hope. "No. I'm in my—"

—REDACTED—

The loud and impersonal voice startled both women.

"Benjamin," Zuri said, slowing her pace. "What was that?"

Ahead of her once more, Benjamin called back. "VainGlory monitors and edits conversations taking place with anyone outside the city. Your friend will see and hear only what the city allows."

"Zuri?" Mae Lin said in dismay. "Are you alright?"

"I'm fine. But I'm being edited."

Mae Lin looked at Zuri as if she'd just announced that a Brontosaurus had stolen her lunch. "What now?"

Zuri explained and then told her friend about the upcoming launch. "What do you think I should use tonight?"

Mae Lin laughed. "I like irony. How about my bubble dress design?"

Of course. Why didn't I think of that?

"Perfect. Just like I told my boss, you're the brains of this operation. I'm going to get you here as soon as I can, but it won't happen until—"

—REDACTED—

Zuri heaved an exasperated sigh at having her conversation edited by the machinations of her Personal Bubble. "Sorry. I wish I could tell you more. Let's just say it might take longer than we thought, but I'm working on it."

"No problem. I have faith in you."

After ending the call, Mae Lin's words haunted Zuri long after she'd dismissed the TalkToMe icon back to its tiny place on the wall of her Personal Bubble.

"We're here!" Benjamin announced happily. "Welcome to your new home."

Zuri squinted at the dim images outside her bubble. "Are we inside?"

"Yes, Miss. We currently stand inside your new home, located on the first floor of the Silver Tower. Your supervisor alluded to the need for you to rise in rank. Any accomplishment will gain you a home higher in this tower. When you reach the highest floor, your next accomplishment will move you into the Gold Tower."

That's what Donna meant when she said Zuri's success would advance her.

She said when I make it to the highest tower, Mae Lin can come to VainGlory. I'm in the Silver Tower now, and the only thing higher than silver is gold. I have to figure out what to do to get into the Gold Tower.

Benjamin stepped front and center into Zuri's field of vision. He spread his robotic arms wide apart, and every image inside her Personal Bubble faded, revealing what appeared to be a living room outside the transparent wall separating her Personal Bubble from the real world. "I have taken the liberty of ordering your lunch, while also enabling all restaurants in VainGlory to recognize you and your delivery address." He gestured toward a small door located in the middle of a long curving wall. "This is where all deliveries will be placed."

The robotic assistant walked to the curving wall and opened the small door to reveal a paper bag marked "Thai Palace." He then gestured toward a corner of the room where Zuri recognized a stack of the boxes she'd packed. "And here are the things you shipped."

Zuri tossed the satchel she carried on top of the pile and sank onto the sofa next to it.

Time to get to work.

"That's all for now, Ben," she said. "I'll call you when I need you."

* * *

That night, Zuri shivered as she walked through the streets of VainGlory. She kept the outside world to a dim outline, while surrounded by the icon tiles of the people and places she loved inside her Personal Bubble, brimming with excited chatter from every direction.

Benjamin walked by her side. "Nothing to worry about, Miss. Do your best, and you'll be fine."

Warm and soothing music swelled around her, as if Zuri stood in the center of an orchestra.

She remembered how Benjamin had told her that her Personal Soundtrack would tell her how to feel. She'd scoffed at the time but now had to admit the music pacified her nerves.

"Here we are," Benjamin said in an encouraging voice. "The Bridge at the Carnival of Animals."

Zuri came to a sudden stop. "Wait. What's wrong with it?"

She dimmed her interior world until the one outside came into better focus.

A line of women and men stood at the foot of the bridge.

"This is the place I chose for my launch," Zuri said to Benjamin in dismay. "These people are blocking my entrance. What are they doing here?" Before Benjamin could respond, Zuri answered her own question. "They must be fans. They don't realize they're in my way."

Zuri rushed to the woman at the end of the line and said, "Excuse me. I need to get through."

Zuri's Personal Soundtrack fell silent except for the ominous undertones of a bassoon.

When the woman turned to face her, Zuri let out a gasp, so startled that she quickly gestured for the outside world to dim and her interior world to dominate. The thought of having to look at the woman's real face made Zuri's stomach turn. "Karen," Zuri said in surprise.

An icon from Zuri's bubble wall came front and center, one she didn't recognize. A label blazed in red neon letters above the doorway that opened on that icon, reading, "In Person."

The scene in the doorway took on the appearance of an Impressionist painting. Zuri recognized the bridge, the Carnival of Animals, and the crystal animals roaming below the bridge. Karen materialized as a wispy figure. "Zuri," Karen said in a sarcastic tone. "I never dreamed I'd see you in VainGlory. Enjoy it while it lasts. I imagine you'll be going home tomorrow."

Glancing beyond Karen, Zuri recognized everyone standing in line, all of them competitors in her business. All of them used to judging each other's work in a snarky way, something Zuri and Mae Lin had long ago agreed to avoid. The way their competitors talked made their skin crawl, and the friends believed joining that talk would make them hate themselves and possibly each other.

Zuri ignored Karen's verbal jabs, still confused by the presence of all her competitors. Had they come to judge her work? Dread filled her to the point where she considered running back home.

But she'd never make it in VainGlory if she ran away from everything that scared her.

Fishing for information, Zuri said, "How did you know I'd be here?"

Karen laughed. "I didn't. It wasn't until I talked to the others that I found out this is a competition."

"Competition?" Zuri said without thinking what the consequences might be. "But this is supposed to be my launch!"

Karen laughed harder. "That's what everybody here was told." She took a long and slow look up and down Zuri's body. "Too bad you didn't bring the best you've got."

Zuri bristled, grateful when her Personal Soundtrack kicked in with blaring, upbeat music. Then she realized the music didn't come from her Personal Soundtrack. The music sounded distant. It came from the world outside her bubble.

Spots of light beamed from high above and crisscrossed over the bridge in time to the melody.

An invisible voice said, "Welcome the new designers of VainGlory!"

One side of the bridge lit up with the name of the man first in line, and he took the cue to strut down the length of the bridge, while the invisible announcer described his work.

Benjamin stepped in front of Zuri's field of view. With lilting hands, he orchestrated the exterior world to fade away so that it was still visible without being overwhelming. Another sweep of his arms brought up the Personal Soundtrack with a composition that complemented the exterior sound but trumped it. "Breathe, Miss," Benjamin said. "Just breathe."

Tears of gratitude and fear welled in Zuri's eyes. She took her Personal Digital Assistant's advice. Taking deep breaths, she became aware of how the music all around her reverberated inside her skin, which calmed her. She sank into that sense of calm, shutting everything else out.

Several minutes later, Benjamin said, "Ready, Miss. You're up."

With a start, Zuri faded her wall of icons and sharpened her view of the outside world enough to recognize Karen completing her walk. Sporting one of her signature pieces, Karen flounced in a bright red coat that acted as if it had a life of its own. The hem levitated like a magician's assistant, its edges tilting from side to side. The center ballooned out and then concaved back to hug her body.

As soon as Karen set foot off the bridge, Zuri breezed past her, forcing confidence into her walk. At first glance, Zuri's slim and full-length black dress appeared to be nothing special. Wearing a keypad glove on one hand, she tapped her fingertips against each other to activate the dress, which now acted like a digital screen, even though it flowed and swayed like cloth. Tiny white spheres came into view at the hem, rising up Zuri's body, like bubbles floating to the top of a flute of champaign.

Striding across the bridge, the sight of the crystal animals below gave her assurance, and she saw an opportunity to show off the dress's potential.

Zuri tapped a new sequence of commands with her fingertips.

The white bubbles turned bright yellow, and then small groups of bubbles took on different colors. The light from each bubble swept like a floodlight until it found a crystal animal below and illuminated it. A dragon roared when it glowed purple. An elephant trumpeted when it lit up orange.

The dusky park below the bridge reminded Zuri of a Christmas tree decorated with lights made of animals.

After casting light inside a dozen animals, she shut off the flooding beams from her dress until only the bubbles floating across its surface held that light.

With another swift command, Zuri brought her Book of Friends front and center inside her Personal Bubble, where dozens of images cheered and shouted encouragement.

A sudden movement outside her bubble caught Zuri's attention, and she looked down.

Water churned in a canal below the far end of the bridge. She thought there must be something in the water, but the moving surface made it impossible to see anything beneath it.

Funny. She hadn't noticed a canal in this park earlier today.

Then again, Zuri had to admit she was in the habit of not noticing a lot of things. After pivoting at the far end of the bridge, she made her triumphant walk back to where she'd entered.

But as soon as Zuri stepped off the bridge, Karen stepped back on for another pass. This time, Karen whipped off her life-of-its-own red coat to reveal a slim beige dress. After taking a few steps, long bristles popped up from the dress, making Karen look like a porcupine.

Zuri withered in defeat as the icons that had previously hailed her now erupted in louder and more vigorous cheers for Karen's reveal. Zuri stared at her competitor, appalled by the woman's nerve.

At the opposite end of the bridge, Karen paused and struck a myriad of poses. Celebrating what she appeared to assume as a clear win, Karen flung her coat over the rail of the bridge and dragged it as she walked back. The porcupine quills of her dress tapped against the clear rails of the bridge like drumsticks.

Zuri's Personal Soundtrack swelled with sorrowful music as if prompting her to assume failure and grieve. Without meaning to, she allowed her heart to sink.

Still at the far end of the bridge, Karen stumbled and fell.

The other competitors surrounding Zuri buzzed with excitement, while Zuri dimmed the wall of icons inside her Personal Bubble so she could get a better look at what was happening outside it.

Still clinging to the red coat draped across the bridge rail, Karen climbed back to her feet and tugged on the coat as if it had snagged on a bolt.

Water splashed in a loud interruption.

A shark leapt over the rail and landed on the bridge. It bit onto the coat and Karen's arm, as she shrieked in terror and tried to get away.

The competitors around Zuri screamed. They ran away from the bridge and back toward the heart of VainGlory.

Benjamin appeared in front of Zuri and brought her icons front and forward, her wall now filled with gaping and trembling fans. "Hurry, Miss! We must get to safety at once!"

Blindly following his direction, Zuri turned her back on the bridge and ran a few steps.

But then a new realization hit her.

The shark wasn't an illusion. It wasn't part of the show. That meant Karen's life was in actual danger.

Zuri waved her hands at the chaotic wall of icons. "Dim!" she commanded. "Mute!"

Obeying, her Personal Bubble became transparent. When Zuri turned to face the bridge, she had a gruesome view of the bridge, Karen, and the shark.

"I must insist!" Benjamin said, appearing in front of her again. "Go home where it's safe!"

"Shut up, Ben," Zuri said. She took off her heels, hiked up her dress, and ran toward Karen and the shark.

Karen's blood spilled across the crystal bridge, making it look like a crime scene suspended in air. Karen screeched and wriggled to get away, the porcupine quills of her dress now dripping red. The shark whipped her against the surface of the bridge as if trying to silence her.

Zuri halted at the edge of the blood to avoid slipping on it.

How do I avoid the shark?

With mindful steps, she advanced. When Zuri tapped her fingertips against each other, she hoped she remembered a command she'd rarely used.

The bubbles on the surface of her dress

glowed white once more, and they cast laser-like beams at the shark's eyes.

The creature shivered but kept its deadly grip on Karen's arm.

Holding one shoe firmly by the toe, Zuri slammed the spike against the shark's skin until it shifted its attention from Karen to Zuri. "Let her go!" Zuri shouted at the shark.

Obliging, the shark released Karen and took aim at Zuri with an open mouth of bloodied teeth.

Keeping the light from her dress beamed at the animal, Zuri rushed closer and punched the shark's eye as hard as she could. The give of its flesh startled her.

It's real.

The shark shuddered but squirmed to get a better angle on Zuri.

Before it could attack, Zuri moved even closer and hit the shark's eye harder with her fist.

Stunned, the shark writhed in pain.

Free of the shark's grip, Karen had begun crawling away.

Zuri took a quick look at Karen.

I don't have the strength to carry her.

Before the shark could regain its senses, Zuri decided on the best course of action. She reached down, wrapped a firm hand around one of Karen's ankles, and hurried toward the other end of the bridge, dragging the other woman behind. The blood on her dress's porcupine quills made the bridge's crystal surface even more slippery, allowing Zuri to pull the injured woman faster. She picked up the pace and tugged Karen to safety.

The shark twisted and jerked on the bridge, unable to find the same kind of purchase.

Now on the park grass, Zuri called out, "Help! Why isn't anyone here to help!"

Benjamin hovered faintly in front of her.

"Ben," Zuri ordered. "Get help now."

He nodded and faded away.

Karen sobbed and trembled, unable to speak. Although her arm was still attached, the shark's bite had mangled it, and blood poured from the wounds.

Zuri reached for Karen's coat, only to realize she'd left it behind. Looking back at the bridge, Zuri saw the shark attack the red coat, a poor substitute for Karen.

With a quick resolve, Zuri assessed everything within reach. She had no extra clothing, only her dress and heels. Even if she could pry off the quills from Karen's dress, she doubted they'd be of any use. And the grass on the ground would be of no help.

Hands. I've got my hands.

First, Zuri sat behind Karen and propped the woman to rest in Zuri's lap, taking a position Zuri knew she could maintain for however long it took for an ambulance to arrive. With gentle hands, she lifted Karen's injured arm. "Don't worry. Help is coming."

Gritting her teeth, Zuri wrapped her hands around the bite marks as a makeshift bandage and applied pressure until the paramedics arrived and whisked Karen away, ignoring Zuri and leaving her standing alone in the Carnival of Animals.

CHAPTER 4

When Zuri arrived home that night, she first stripped off her ruined dress in the bathroom and took a shower to wash the blood from her skin. She discovered her folded pajamas on top of a hamper in the bathroom, grateful to slip into them. She wandered into the living room and sank onto the sofa, staring into mid-air in a daze.

Although the harsh edges of her apartment reminded her of the awful reality she'd faced earlier tonight, she kept her wall of icons dimmed, unable to bear the chaos.

For once, she wanted silence.

Tonight, Zuri had managed to do what no designer should ever do.

Her profession demanded the show of elitism. All competitors had to act like enemies in order to make customers choose sides, which had been proven to increase sales. The designers who had run away from the shark attack had done what was expected of them. One less designer in their midst meant less competition.

Helping Karen had been akin to professional suicide.

Benjamin appeared faintly. "If you don't mind, Miss, I thought you could use some comfort." He gestured to the small door in the center of the living room wall, the one designated for food delivery.

Zuri's stomach rumbled, and it encouraged her to walk to the door and open it.

Inside sat a canister in a bed of fog. "What is this?"

"I understand your favorite flavor is mint chocolate chip."

Zuri opened the chilled canister to find a pint of ice cream inside.

And a spoon.

Zuri resumed her position on the sofa, quiet until she ate the entire pint. "Thank you, Ben. For the ice cream and for calling the paramedics."

"Of course, Miss." Still appearing as a faint outline, he took a tentative seat next to her on the sofa. "Every interaction we have helps me learn about you so that I may become of better service. If you don't mind, Miss, why did you do it?"

With a heavy sigh, Zuri put the empty ice cream container on the nearby coffee table. "I guess I was hungrier than I thought."

"Not the ice cream, Miss. The woman. The shark."

Zuri looked at him. "Come forward, Ben."

The silver robot sharpened its appearance from a faint outline until he looked present and real. "Miss? I thought that woman was your rival. Wouldn't it have been in your best interest to run home when I told you?"

"You can't just let people die, Ben."

"But she hurt your feelings. She said terrible things to you, and she's been doing it for years."

Zuri shrugged. "I might have walked away if she were a serial killer or a despot who tortures people. But that's not who Karen is. She can be mean, but she's not dangerous." Tears welled in Zuri's eyes.

"Is she someone special to you?"

If Benjamin had been real, Zuri would have made an excuse and brushed his question off with a laugh. But here in the privacy of her home—and in the wake of a terrible night that still left her hands shaking—Zuri caved in to the luxury of telling him the truth. "Not Karen. When I first got into this business, I was 14 and on my own for the first time. I met another designer online and we became friends. But she climbed fast and left for VainGlory. I spent too much time envying her instead of having fun with her. And then, three months later, she vanished. No one knows what happened, and it dawned on me that I'd never see her again. I wasted all that time envying her success when I could have stayed in touch. And if I'd done that, maybe she never would have disappeared. Or, at least, I might have had a clue what happened to her."

"I'm sorry, Miss."

"That's why Mae Lin is so important to me. It's why I have to get her to VainGlory, so we can succeed together. And that's why Karen doesn't bother me. Maybe only a handful of people get to the top, but it's possible we can all get there sooner or later."

"I take it your other competitors don't think so. They ran away."

"That's their choice, Ben. They're the ones who have to live with the consequences, not me." Zuri groaned. "Speaking of which, it was nice knowing you. I guess I'll be kicked out of VainGlory tomorrow."

Although Benjamin's face remained firm and metallic, sadness edged his voice. "I suppose so, Miss. VainGlory keeps a low profile. If you had run home as I suggested instead of helping your rival, that would have helped the city distract fans and convince them the designer launch had unfolded as planned."

"I made a mess of it," Zuri said, realizing her dream had been shattered before it had barely begun. "I drew attention to Karen and the shark instead of letting the city gloss over what happened." She paused and frowned. "Benjamin, why would the city put a shark in a canal in the Carnival of Animals park?"

"I can't say that I know, Miss," Benjamin said. "But I'm certain the city has its reasons."

A familiar ringtone that sounded like a rainstorm startled Zuri. "Mae Lin." She hesitated, failing to answer.

A voice rang above the ringtone. "Zuri, where are you? I can't find you anywhere. Answer me!"

It's my fault. I made a mess of everything. It's not just my dream I destroyed—it's Mae Lin's, too.

Zuri wanted to run away and hide so no one could find her. She wanted to crawl into bed and pull the covers over her head. She wanted to be left alone so she'd never have to speak to anyone ever again.

Mae Lin's ringtone changed to the sound of her voice saying, "Answer me ... answer me ... answer me."

For a moment, Zuri considered taking the contacts out of her eyes in order to get out of her Personal Bubble. That way, she wouldn't be able to hear any ring tones, much less answer any calls.

But that would mean a total disconnect from the world. Zuri would have no idea what was happening at any of her favorite places. She'd be out of the public eye instead of taking a brief break from it.

What if something important happens, and I'm not there to know about it?

Zuri braced herself. She couldn't blame Mae Lin's disappointment or anger or dismay. Zuri would have to endure it.

She answered the call, and Mae Lin's face floated directly in front of Zuri.

But Mae Lin didn't look disappointed or angry or dismayed.

She looked excited and happy.

"Zuri!" Mae Lin shouted. "What happened at the launch?"

Without thinking, Zuri began to explain, "Karen took a second walk."

"Yes, I saw her do that, but then everything was redacted. It filled my screen with overlapping black squares. I couldn't make out anything."

Of course. VainGlory wouldn't let anything so horrific go beyond the city limits.

Zuri tried to explain. "When Karen came walking back, there was a—"

—REDACTED—

"Shark?" Mae Lin said breathlessly. "Was there a shark?"

With a start, Zuri realized that VainGlory appeared to have the power to edit her end of the conversation but had no control over what Mae Lin said.

Zuri gave a quick nod, hoping it would slip past before VainGlory could redact it.

"Haven't you seen what people are saying?" Mae Lin continued, beside herself with excitement.

Zuri hung her head in shame. "I don't want to."

"Look!" Mae Lin said. "You have to look."

Trusting her friend, Zuri grimaced as she brought her wall of icons back into view. The images waved and shouted for her attention.

Zuri returned her attention to Mae Lin, whose face still displayed front and center. "I thought everyone would hate me."

Mae Lin laughed. "Not likely. Take a look."

One by one, Zuri brought up the icons of her favorite places alongside the image of Mae Lin, surprised to see various emojis of sharks flipping belly up, getting black eyes, and suffering broken teeth. The icons began shouting, "Let her go! Let her go! Let her go!"

Zuri looked at Mae Lin in confusion. "I don't get it."

"I guess it didn't get redacted in VainGlory. The people who live there are talking about it everywhere. No images are getting out, but people started talking about you before anyone thought to stop them." Mae

Lin paused to catch her breath. "I don't know exactly what you did, but I'm getting the gist."

Sitting back in disbelief, Zuri said, "I thought it would ruin me and you both."

"You thought wrong. Orders are pouring in. So far, we've made more in the last hour than in the last ten years."

More stunned by the moment, Zuri said, "What?"

"All of our fans want the black dress you wore. But most orders are from new customers—people in VainGlory. They want the 'shark killer dress.'"

A new thought made the back of Zuri's throat go cold. "If we're getting that many orders, how long will they take to fill?"

Mae Lin grinned. "It's no problem for our regulars. They know how long it takes for me to print the dress and ship it. But all of the VainGlory people want to print the dress at home. All of the VainGlory orders are filled automatically. Think of it, Zuri. I'm not the only one using the code you wrote to print the dress. Everyone in VainGlory is buying your code!"

Something Mae Lin said earlier finally registered with Zuri. "You said we already made more tonight than in the last ten years? How is that possible?"

"Remember how you told me to charge ten times the dress price for the code that prints it? I didn't. I'm charging 100 times, and we're getting thousands of orders from VainGlorians." Mae Lin reached off-screen, pulled in a bottle of champaign, and popped the cork. The alcohol gushed out, and she took a big gulp. "Here's to us!"

Even in terms of VainGlory wealth, tonight's success had to be big, especially if orders were still pouring in.

"That's it," Zuri said, more to herself than to Mae Lin. "It's what I need to get into the Gold Tower."

"Tower? There are towers in VainGlory?"

Focusing on Mae Lin, Zuri said, "Yes. My supervisor said once I get to the highest tower, you can come to VainGlory. And this has to be big enough to get me into the Gold Tower."

The excitement on Mae Lin's face faded. "Does that matter anymore? We now have enough to get what we want. I'll get my own house, free and clear, and so will you. What's left over will be the kind of nest egg to last a lifetime."

Zuri brushed off that idea. "Who wants to settle for that when we can get even more rich and famous here in VainGlory?" Her mind raced. "Who knows where this will lead? Remember all those years when we dreamed about making it to the top? The top is right here in VainGlory."

Mae Lin took another swig of champaign. "I guess. I say let's sleep on it and talk again in the morning." She raised the bottle in triumph and then blinked out.

For the next several hours, Zuri bounced in and out of all her favorite places, awash in the glow of overnight success for which she and Mae Lin had spent the last ten years preparing.

CHAPTER 5

Zuri slept deeply that night, feeling fresh and renewed when she came awake.

Still surrounded by the icons filling the round wall of her Personal Bubble, Zuri noticed many of them were covered with "Z"s to indicate few people currently visited those places. For the first time, she noticed a Sound icon located above her head on the wall, covered with an "X" to show Zuri had all sound muted for now.

Moments after opening her eyes, Zuri blinked in surprise when the image of her Personal Digital Assistant hovered above her bed. "Good morning, Miss. I have quite a lot of good news to tell you."

Apparently, Benjamin had the ability to override her Mute.

Zuri sat up in bed. She clutched the sheets to her chest, even though she wore her favorite pajamas, a background of bamboo shoots dotted with pandas. "Ben, please. I just woke up."

The image shifted so that it appeared to sit on the far end of her bed. "I understand, Miss. But the news is quite exciting. I thought you'd want to hear."

Last night's success came back to Zuri like a picture coming into focus. "Right. So, go ahead and tell me."

Benjamin's amber eyes glowed brighter. "You have been moved to the top of the Silver Tower! That means you're one step away from moving to the Gold Tower."

Forgetting any inclination toward modesty, Zuri jumped out of bed. "Great! When do we move? Do I have time to get dressed?"

"Move?" Benjamin's eyes blinked. "We're already there."

"We can't be. I moved onto the first floor yesterday." She squinted at Benjamin. "We were still on the first floor when I went to bed last night, right?"

"Of course. But during the night, we were moved to the top of the tower." Benjamin stood and gestured for her to follow him. "Come see."

Not believing him, Zuri grabbed a robe and shrugged into it as she hurried to keep pace.

Benjamin opened a door from the living room and walked out. "Remember to dim your bubble so you can see."

"Right," Zuri muttered to herself. She waved a hand to fade the icons enough to see through her bubble wall and detect the world outside it. Her apartment looked the same. She didn't know if it had actually moved or if everything inside—including her sleeping self—had been moved during the night. If, in fact, Benjamin told her the truth, which she assumed he must always do.

Zuri caught her breath when she walked through the open door and onto a balcony that gave her a bird's-eye view of the city below. She joined Benjamin at the balcony rail and clung to it. "We must be 50 stories high!"

Benjamin corrected her. "Fifty-eight. If you look up, Miss, you'll see there are none above us. You have indeed climbed to the top of the Silver Tower. And in just one day!"

Zuri craned her neck. Just as Benjamin said, her floor stood the highest with only the building's roof above it.

The wall of her Personal Bubble vibrated all around her, and Zuri turned to Benjamin for answers.

"You currently have everything—except for me, of course—on Mute. When all is Muted, your bubble will vibrate to signal that an official of VainGlory requests your immediate attention."

Zuri rushed back inside, not wanting to

risk forgetting her surroundings and falling over the rail by accident. Straightening her robe, she turned the Sound back on.

"Good morning, Zuri," Donna's voice said.

In her haste, Zuri had forgotten to dim the outside world. She now waved away the interior of her home and brought forward her icon wall.

The Incoming Connect icon came forward, where the image of a musical note gave way to the cartoon caterpillar that Donna had presented yesterday during another call. This time, her caterpillar shape took an orange hue dotted with black. Its delicate black legs investigated a pile of bright green leaves. "Your success has been quite surprising."

Zuri couldn't tell if Donna meant those words as a compliment or criticism. "I'm surprised, too."

"I've monitored your sales, which are still trickling in. Your sales alone have been enough to lift you to the heights of Silver." The black-dotted orange caterpillar chewed the center out of a leaf. "If you were to manage getting your first Endorsement today, that would qualify a move to Gold." The caterpillar swallowed a mouthful of leaf. "First floor, of course, but Gold nonetheless."

"I have plenty of endorsements from before. I can show you."

The caterpillar chuckled. "Those hold no weight in VainGlory. The Endorsement I speak of must come from within the city, not outside it. Such an Endorsement is not easy to achieve, although I think you're perfectly positioned if you act quickly."

Zuri sat up straighter, her interest sharpened. "How? What do I do?"

"The spillover interest from last night makes it possible to promote a new product that can be seen as a companion to your successful one. The Bubble Brella, the equivalent of an umbrella for the Personal Bubble." With dainty jerks, the caterpillar stripped one side of the leaf from its spine. "Take it to the water garden, where a shark will attempt to attack you."

Zuri froze in fright. "You want a shark to kill me?"

The caterpillar laughed. "Of course not. It will be a simulation, not a real shark."

Zuri sagged with relief. "So, I'll tell people the umbrella keeps out simulations."

"No," the caterpillar said. "Everyone must believe the shark is real. The only reason I'm telling you it's a simulation is so you know you'll be safe."

Zuri shifted her weight, suddenly uncomfortable. "But if a real shark attacked me when I had the umbrella over my bubble, would I be safe?"

The caterpillar stripped away the other

side of the leaf and dropped the empty stem. "It's doubtful."

"If I don't tell people the shark is just a simulation, they'll assume they'll be safe if a shark attacks them. But they won't be. They could be killed."

"No one is going to be attacked by a shark."

Zuri didn't like disagreeing with anyone. It made her feel pained and distressed. But lying made her feel worse.

"Karen was attacked by a shark last night. It tried to attack me, too."

The caterpillar stuffed the stripped bits of leaf into its mouth until it bulged. "That was an anomaly. Every so often, the network that runs VainGlory experiences an unexpected glitch. Last night, there was a glitch in the security wall surrounding the island, which allowed a shark from the ocean to infiltrate our canals. The glitch has been fixed. Nothing like that will ever happen again."

Zuri wavered. Before coming to VainGlory, she'd made her own decisions—or made them with Mae Lin. They'd never seen any reason to lie about anything for any reason. They'd achieved their greatest successes by telling the truth.

No one had ever told Zuri to lie before now. And she didn't like the idea of lying to new customers. Her fan base would be appalled if she lied to them.

"But won't people get upset if they find out I lied?" Zuri said.

The caterpillar spoke with its mouth open, and tiny bits of chewed grass fell out. "Not in VainGlory. It doesn't matter."

Zuri found that hard to believe, but VainGlory had surprised her at every turn. When she'd rescued Karen from the shark, Zuri assumed that would be the end of her career. She thought she'd be kicked out of the city.

Life in VainGlory was very different from anything she'd experienced before. Maybe lying was expected here. Maybe people living in VainGlory truly didn't mind.

"All right," Zuri said with reluctance. "When do I go?"

"Now." The caterpillar swallowed everything in its mouth. "You'll be provided with everything you need when you get to the water garden. Your PDA will help you."

The image of the caterpillar winked out of sight, and the Incoming Connect icon automatically reduced back to its place on the bubble wall.

Benjamin shimmered briefly.

Worried, Zuri said, "Are you alright?"

His eyes burned bright. "Nothing to worry about. Simply an update." He pointed toward her bedroom. "You should wear what you wore last night. It will provide the greatest impact."

Zuri nodded her agreement and walked

into her bedroom, leaving the image of Benjamin outside.

She'd learned over the years to grab every opportunity that presented itself, because some only come around once.

But she couldn't ignore the way her stomach now twisted into knots.

CHAPTER 6

A short time later, Zuri walked through the city and then into the Carnival of Animals park. She kept her wall of icons vivid, while making her bubble wall just translucent enough for her to recognize her location and keep her bearings. Every minute or so, she dimmed one icon and brought a different one front and center in order to examine or interact with it. Her Soundtrack played bright music with optimistic lyrics. Zuri hummed along.

Benjamin kept pace at her side. "If you don't mind the suggestion, Miss, this might be a good time to keep a sharper eye on the outside."

"Why?"

If Benjamin hadn't been a thing composed at the core of nothing more than ones and zeroes, Zuri would have thought a smile crept into his voice. "I believe it would be to your benefit."

Even in her old life, Zuri preferred the screen to the world beyond it. Shutting out the harshness of the real world made her feel safe and comforted. Normally, she dreaded any contact with it, except for spending time with Mae Lin.

But Benjamin's sly suggestion piqued her curiosity. Zuri thrust one hand toward the wall to push it into the background before commanding her bubble wall to become transparent enough to see through it.

It took a moment for Zuri to figure out where she stood. Looking back, she saw the bridge behind her. She stood on one of many paths winding through the park where crystal animals mimicked grazing on real grass.

When she'd first walked through the park, Zuri and Donna had been the only people here. Last night, Zuri had been surrounded by other designers. Otherwise, they'd been alone.

But now, dozens of people filled the walkways.

Even more surprising, every one of them, men and women alike, wore the same dress as Zuri.

Mae Lin's bubble dress.

Zuri's copy had self-cleaned overnight, although a few small rust-colored spots remained, remnants of Karen's blood from where the shark bit her arm and dripped onto Zuri's dress.

Zuri shrank in fear, not wanting to be recognized because she didn't like talking to strangers. "Ben," she whispered, "get me out of here!"

Although his metallic face bore no expression, his amber eyes blinked, appearing startled. "Why?"

Zuri kept her voice low, frantic to make sure no one overheard her. "They'll recognize me from last night. I have a job, and I can't be interrupted before I get that job done."

Benjamin's voice brightened. "Nothing to worry about, Miss! Everyone in VainGlory lives inside a Personal Bubble of their own. Like you, few have the patience for allowing the outside world to distract them. I dare say that no one knows you're here. After all, they'd have to look outside their bubbles to notice you."

Zuri's Soundtrack played a bouncy and fun tune. She noticed how it seemed to lift her spirits. "Are you sure? No one will see me?"

"Quite unlikely, Miss."

Zuri's Soundtrack made her feel brazen. She decided to test Benjamin's claim. "Is it possible to make my bubble wall go invisible? Can you show me how?"

"Certainly." With a flick of his robotic

wrist, Benjamin eliminated the appearance of the wall surrounding Zuri.

She felt naked to the real world, wrapping her arms around her chest as if to protect herself from prying eyes.

But just as Benjamin said, no eyes pried.

Instead, every person stood or walked alone, talking or laughing or pausing to record a selfie with one of the animals.

A short distance in front of Zuri, a tall man had adapted Mae Lin's design so that the bubble dress wrapped around his waist, leaving his muscular chest bare, covered with swirling tattoos. Against the black background, large white bubbles floated across his dress-skirt like helium balloons trapped inside a small room. The same tattoos on his chest suddenly appeared on each white bubble. He reminded Zuri of an ancient warrior.

Zuri's Soundtrack music swelled, and her courage followed suit. She took a slow walk toward the tall man, staring at him the entire time.

He failed to see her, even when Zuri passed by, mere inches away.

A crystal deer trotted toward Zuri, followed by a woman wearing her adapted version of Mae Lin's dress: instead of flowing past her ankles, the dress climbed high above her knees. Tiny violet bubbles spelled out the words "See me!"

When the crystal deer darted away to avoid colliding with Zuri, the woman did likewise. However, she babbled the entire time, never knowing Zuri was there.

A brief moment of worry tugged at Zuri, far beneath the luster of her Soundtrack.

Is that what I look like when I'm in my bubble? Do I get that oblivious?

Despite the absence of her bubble wall, Benjamin still projected at her side. "We should move on. We're expected to be on time."

Zuri hustled through the Carnival of Animals and then the Animated Garden full of vibrant flowers until she entered the water garden. The rain-like sounds from the various fountains surrounding her relaxed Zuri. She looked at Benjamin. "Now what?"

"It's best if you keep your wall down for now. The words will appear in front of you. All you need do is say them out loud."

Zuri's Soundtrack intensified, and she realized it now played outside as well as inside her bubble. Bright white words floated in the air in front of her. Taking the cue from Benjamin, she read them out loud.

"I'm alright," Zuri said, "because I'm under my Bubble Brella."

Her Soundtrack played a chorus of women singing, "I'm alright, because I'm under my Bubble Brella."

All the fountains within range of Zuri

turned their streams of water at her. Before she could react, water fell like raindrops down the invisible curved wall of her Personal Bubble. Zuri remained dry.

More words floated in the air, and Zuri spoke them out loud. "See? It's an umbrella for my Personal Bubble."

The Soundtrack chorus sang, "See how dry she is! She has an umbrella for her bubble."

Benjamin gestured for Zuri to follow him to stand beside a canal whose surface churned slightly.

What if Donna lied to me? What if it's a real shark? What if it kills me?

Zuri took a calming breath.

None of that made sense. Zuri's launch had been a great success. She'd met Donna's expectations. Wouldn't Donna stand to lose if she let anything bad happen to Zuri?

The Soundtrack chorus repeated its refrain, which inspired Zuri to move forward. Once more, she read floating words. "Nothing can hurt me under my Bubble Brella."

Zuri forced herself to smile strong and resist flinching when a shark launched out of the canal and struck the invisible umbrella with so much force that she felt the reverberations throughout her entire body.

It looked real enough to her. Could a projected image of a shark shake her to the core?

The shark's face flattened against the clear wall, and the animal slid down it and back into the canal.

The Soundtrack chorus sang, "Not even a shark can get me under my Bubble Brella!"

Zuri balked at the words "I'm invincible" floating before her eyes. She opened her mouth, unwilling to say the words.

What happened next wasn't so much a conscious decision as a visceral one. Zuri spoke without thinking.

"Even if a shark could break through, I'd punch it in the eye!"

For a few moments, the Soundtrack chorus remained silent. But then the chorus followed Zuri's lead instead of singing the scripted words. "We'd punch it in the eye!"

The round wall of icons inside Zuri's bubble lit up as if it were ablaze. In rapid-fire succession, one icon after another came front and center, each touting Zuri and the Bubble Brella. Every icon showed some form of approval, ranging from cartoon images representing that icon as it punched a comical shark to replays of Zuri punching last night's shark or her Bubble Brella repelling one moments ago.

As one icon replaced another, a bright gold light framed the previous icon when it minimized back to its place on the wall.

The image of a fist holding a stamp

punched a bright red badge reading "Approved!" on every gold-framed icon so fast that it sounded like a machine gun.

The Soundtrack singers broke into a rendition of the Hallelujah Chorus as an orchestra swelled beneath their voices.

Stunned with surprise and happiness, a lump formed in Zuri's throat while she stared in wonder at the bright golden light filling the interior of her bubble.

Zuri felt as if she'd just arrived at the gates of heaven.

A sign reading "Bubble Brella sales" displayed above the highest row of icons alongside a counter with the number zero. In an instant, the number flipped over and climbed like a rocket into the hundreds, the thousands, the tens of thousands. When the number passed the 100,000 mark, the image of a bottle of champaign hovered below the counter, and its cork popped like a loud cannon.

While the counter number continued to climb, a sparkling white banner unfurled below the champaign bottle and across the width of Zuri's field of vision. While horns trumpeted, black words scrolled across the banner like a stock-market ticker: *Breaking Trend! Breaking Trend! Breaking Trend!*

The Soundtrack chorus stopped singing "Hallelujah" and instead shouted, "Congratulations! You have achieved Gold Tower status!"

Overwhelmed by her unexpected success, Zuri wept, unsure whether she cried out of happiness or fear or both.

CHAPTER 7

Zuri regretted spending her time relishing accolades once Benjamin led her into her new home on the ground floor of the Gold Tower, wishing she'd watched their approach to the building instead of being distracted by her new fans in VainGlory. She dimmed the wall of icons to inspect the apartment. Confused, she said, "This looks like the Silver Tower. Are you sure we're in Gold?"

"Positively, Miss," Benjamin said. "Follow me to see for yourself."

Her Digital Personal Assistant opened a door in the living room wall and led her to a portico outside. He pointed to a curving line of silver towers a few blocks away. "The Silver Towers form a ring around the Gold Towers. If you turn around and look at the exterior of this building, you can verify its color."

Sure enough, when Zuri checked the exterior of the tower, it shimmered a golden yellow. "I'm on the ground floor."

Benjamin lifted his metallic shoulders in the best shrug he could manage. "Everyone must start at the bottom, Miss."

The interior of her bubble vibrated with an instrumental snippet of the Hallelujah Chorus.

At first assuming it to be her Personal Soundtrack, Zuri realized with a start that it must be an Incoming Connect, gestured that icon to come forward, and answered it.

A fattened zebra-striped caterpillar sat on its enormous haunches in the middle of a tall pile of vibrant autumn leaves. When its mouth moved, Donna's voice said, "Congratulations, Zuri."

The cold tone of her supervisor's voice worried Zuri. Had they met in person or if Donna had displayed her human face, Zuri would have frozen with dread.

But the sight of the caterpillar reaching for a vivid yellow leaf while straining to keep its precarious balance on the pile eased Zuri's nervousness. She dared to explore her concern by asking a direct question. "Did I do something wrong?"

The silence that followed made Zuri feel sick at her stomach. Still, she held fast and waited for an answer.

"Your job is to follow the script," Donna

said, her caterpillar image struggling at the threat of losing balance. Triumphant in staying on top of the pile, its lower legs pulled the yellow leaf up toward its mouth. Before taking its first bite, the caterpillar said, "You must always follow the script. No exceptions."

At first, Zuri didn't understand.

Then she remembered the words prompted at her when the Bubble Brella surrounded her in the water garden.

I'm invincible.

The words had rubbed her the wrong way, feeling like a lie. Zuri had already stretched her sensibilities thin by pretending the Bubble Brella protected her from a real shark, when she knew it had been nothing more than a simulation.

Back home in the city of Aspire, Zuri and Mae Lin always agreed they'd never lie to their fans. People who lived in Aspire worked hard for their money and had to think carefully before spending it, especially on the kind of luxuries Mae Lin designed.

Like everyone else in Aspire, Zuri hated buying something only to realize she'd been duped into thinking it was something it wasn't. Zuri never wanted any of her fans to feel that way.

A new thought struck Zuri.

Maybe people in VainGlory were different. They had plenty of money and probably didn't know what to do with it. Maybe they didn't mind being duped.

Or maybe they never noticed.

"Remember," Donna said. "Fame is the name of the game."

After all, no one had complained about the Bubble Brella yet, and Zuri was convinced it couldn't hold back any sharks.

But Donna had said the shark that attacked Karen had been an anomaly. If sharks rarely came into VainGlory from the ocean—and why would they want to, anyway—then it must be highly doubtful that anyone would ever be attacked by one again, Bubble Brella or no Bubble Brella.

"I understand," Zuri said. "I promise I'll stick to the script from now on."

"Good," the caterpillar said. By taking tiny bites from the yellow leaf, it had created the shape of a tower inside it. "You achieved Breaking Trend status much sooner than I expected. That's good."

"Yes," Zuri said. "Can Mae Lin get an apartment next to mine?"

The caterpillar still held onto the yellow leaf but let it drift away from its mouth. "Mae Lin?"

"My business partner. You said when I move into the Gold Tower, Mae Lin can come to VainGlory." Zuri gestured at the nearby gleaming wall of the new tower where she lived.

"What I said was when you advance to the highest tower, it will be acceptable to invite your partner to VainGlory."

"But I'm in the Gold Tower now. There's nothing higher than gold."

"Platinum," Donna said in a cool voice. "The highest tower is platinum. But you are well on your way."

Zuri stared at the caterpillar in disbelief, shocked and disappointed.

"I suspect you misunderstood," Benjamin whispered to Zuri. "Or perhaps you assumed."

"What you must focus on next is getting endorsements from people who matter," Donna continued, her caterpillar image resuming its leafy breakfast. "Those endorsements will link together in clusters, and those clusters will give you greater visibility in the Personal Bubbles of Vain-Glorians. As your clusters grow in number, your rank will rise. Breaking trends will also give you top placement in bubbles. Once you achieve breaking trends in niche groups, you'll find it easier to achieve them in the mainstream of VainGlory." The caterpillar paused for effect. "That's how you can make your way to the Platinum Towers."

Too stunned to answer, Zuri simply stared at her supervisor.

"Enough for now," the caterpillar said. It blinked out of sight, and the Incoming Connect icon diminished back to its place on Zuri's wall.

"I don't understand," Zuri said. In the

safety and privacy of her new home, she let herself sink to the verge of tears. "Why does everything have to be so hard?"

"If I may," Benjamin said as he maneuvered to face her. "This is nothing to take personally, Miss. Everyone who comes to VainGlory must do exactly as Miss Donna explained. I see no reason why you can't succeed."

Zuri slumped back inside and threw herself onto the living room sofa in despair. "But there's so much to do! Endorsements. Clusters. Breaking trends. How am I supposed to get any of those?"

Benjamin sat next to her. "This is no time to despair. You only just arrived in VainGlory yesterday, and look at how much you have achieved already!"

Zuri snapped at him in a bitter voice. "Not enough."

"On the contrary, I must insist. Last night, you began as one of several new designers introduced to VainGlory. When your colleague attempted to steal the show—and took the misstep of putting herself in harm's way—you're the one who saved her life. As a result, you're the one that all of VainGlory noticed. People even remembered you this morning, which in itself is quite a feat of accomplishment. Then when you promoted the Bubble Brella, you caught the city's attention yet again with your witticism. Miss Zuri, you are as well positioned for success as anyone who has lived for merely one day in Vain-Glory could be!"

Zuri's mood softened. "I suppose. But I don't know anything about what Donna wants me to do next. And that means I don't know how to do my job."

"As your Personal Digital Assistant, it is my duty to help you with that."

Zuri gave him a sharp look. "You can do that? You can help me with my job?"

Benjamin's silver face maintained its unemotional expression, and his amber eyes flickered briefly. "Why, of course, Miss. I have witnessed many people fail in Vain-Glory, but I have also witnessed others succeed. My data shows that those who make the most personal connections succeed."

Without warning, bright white sparks ignited around him. The silver robot cried out and reached for Zuri before he collapsed and slid off the sofa to the floor.

"Ben!" Zuri cried. Even though she knew he appeared as an image and had no physical presence, she fell to the floor next to him and tried to hold his twitching hand. "What's wrong?"

The robot's amber eyes blinked once and then faded to black.

Zuri stared at him in horror. He'd been on the verge of guiding her through the confusing maze of VainGlory, and now he appeared dead. Or disconnected. Or infected with a virus.

Zuri looked up at her wall of icons and scanned them. Surely, there had to be one for maintenance or repair.

Zuri paused, and tears spilled down her face.

In the short time she'd been in Vain-Glory, Benjamin had been the closest thing she'd had to a friend, even if he was just a program.

He was *her* program, and she wanted his companionship.

She needed it.

A whirring sound caught Zuri's attention. Looking back at Benjamin, she saw his robot body shudder. His eyes came alive with light again, even though they now looked pale green instead of amber.

"Ben!" Zuri cried out with joy. Still crying, she said, "I thought I'd lost you! Are you alright? Is there anything I can do to help you? Should I call someone to help you?"

Benjamin sat up next to Zuri on the floor. He stared at her for a long time. "Zuri."

His loss of formality startled Zuri, but she took it as a compliment.

Maybe this is the moment where our friendship begins. He's no longer just my Personal Digital Assistant. He's my friend.

"How do you feel?" Zuri reconsidered

her question. "Does it make sense for me to ask you that?"

"It makes sense." Benjamin shook his head as if expecting something to rattle inside it. "I'm OK."

Zuri reached out and placed her hands as if they were holding his. "You scared me. I need you. I want you to be with me. I don't think I can do this without you."

Benjamin looked at her hands, appearing to hold his. "Why are you here?"

Zuri didn't know what to make of his question at first. But then she remembered that, moments ago, Ben said the people who make the most personal connections in VainGlory succeed.

That's what he's doing. He's helping me figure out how to make personal connections. He needs to know more about me to do that.

"I want to be famous."

Benjamin's pale green gaze remained strong and steady. "Why? What good will fame do you?"

If Ben had been human, Zuri would have been shocked by the question.

He's a program. He has no way of understanding unless I spell it out for him.

Zuri gathered her thoughts, wanting to help Ben know her better. "Fame is everything. When you're famous, people recognize you right away. They know who you are."

"Why do you need so many people to know you? Isn't family enough?"

Zuri stiffened. "I have no family."

"That isn't what the records show."

His response startled Zuri. She'd been very specific when she'd filled out her application for VainGlory. She'd listed her family status as "orphan."

They must have accessed my records in Aspire.

Normally, Zuri would have responded with a snarky comment, but she knew Ben meant to help her. He needed to know the truth. "I listed my status as an orphan because I feel like one."

Benjamin's voice softened. "Why? What happened to make you feel that way?"

Zuri shrugged, even though she had no problem knowing the answers to his question. "When people treat you like you don't exist, you might as well be an orphan."

"How did that happen? Who did it? What exactly did they do?"

Zuri's voice became scratchy. "My parents acted like they didn't know I was alive." She gestured to the curved wall surrounding her. "They were always too busy with their phones to notice me. It's like they lived in their own Personal Bubble decades before Personal Bubbles existed." She paused and flinched at a memory. "When I was a little girl, we went to one of the old-time places that are supposed to be nostalgic. They had all these weird things, like people dressed up as the tooth fairy or Santa Claus or the Easter Bunny. There was an Easter egg hunt, and kids were running all over the place, trying to find the biggest egg, because whoever found it would win a gigantic stuffed toy. While the other kids were running, I started poking around and found it." Zuri stopped and looked away.

"Go on."

"I was five years old, but I saw a toddler girl who had just seen the big egg, too. I wanted the egg for myself, but that toddler's face lit up with so much joy that it made me happier to let her get it. So, I stayed put and watched her." Zuri's voice stiffened. "That's when my parents—who for once decided to look at me—called to me from the sidelines and told me to let the toddler have the egg." She shook her head in disgust. "They didn't see that I'd already decided to do it. Afterwards, they took credit for what I did. That's what they did all the time, over and over and over again. They never knew me. They didn't see me."

Benjamin's tone stayed even and calm. "Some people would say it was just an Easter egg hunt. They might think you're too sensitive."

"Things like that happened all the time," Zuri said in a quiet voice. "Once when we were walking down a street, I walked slower to see if they'd notice I wasn't there. When I fell two blocks behind, a man across the street gave me a look that made my skin crawl, so I walked faster to catch up to my parents. By the time I did, I could tell they never saw I wasn't walking with them. But what if I'd been kidnapped by that creep? Molested? Murdered?" She paused. "My folks made me feel like a thing. Like I was just a possession to them, not a daughter. I didn't even feel human when I was with them."

With a start, Zuri realized that she'd just told her Personal Digital Assistant that she'd left her family because they'd made her feel inhuman. She'd never heard of a program that had feelings, but her automatic response was to worry that she might have hurt Benjamin's feelings. Even though she doubted she needed to address a possible faux pax, Zuri wanted to be on the safe side with him. "I didn't mean to knock being a non-human. It's just that I am a human, and I don't like it when people act like I'm not."

"I understand," Benjamin said.

"I guess what hurts the most is that they never had any idea who I am. They assumed they knew me, but they didn't."

"Wasn't there anyone else who did?"

Zuri resisted his question at first, wanting to forget her past instead of remember it. But this was for her own good. This was how Ben could help her. "I had an older brother, Rameen. He saw what happened at the Easter egg hunt, and he yelled at our folks and tried to make them understand." Zuri shook her head. "But they never listened to him either. So, he left."

"He must have had his reasons."

"Sure," Zuri said. "He got out and started his own life. That's what I learned from him. You've got nobody in life except yourself, so you'd better start looking out for yourself as soon as you can."

"Oh, Zuri," Benjamin whispered.

"Look, I got out when I was 14. That was ten years ago, and I doubt that anyone ever noticed I'd left." Zuri gathered her thoughts and cooled her emotions. "But the past is the past. I have a good life that's getting better by the moment. And I've got Mae Lin. She's like the sister I never had. She's my family now."

Benjamin stared at her with his blank metallic face. His green eyes seemed to pale.

"So," Zuri continued. "How can we use that? What can we gather from my past that will help me get endorsements and clusters and breaking trends?"

"Are you sure that's what you want to do? Is it possible VainGlory isn't good for you? Would you ever consider returning to your family?"

Zuri looked at Benjamin in horror, but then his words sparked an idea. "Ben!" Zuri said in excitement. "I know what to do."

CHAPTER 8

Riding her new wave of excitement, Zuri waved the Outgoing Connect icon front and center on her bubble. Moments later, Mae Lin's image hovered in the air. Her eyes looked puffy and her face drawn and pale.

"Mae Lin," Zuri said. "What's wrong?"

Her friend spoke in a strained voice. "Another rash of suicides. We lost Ann at the Flower Fairy."

Not believing her, Zuri pushed the image of Mae Lin to the side to make room for a new icon. But when Zuri brought up the Flower Fairy icon, she found it draped with black banners reading "Rest in Peace." Zuri slumped against the back of the sofa. Had she not already been sitting, she would have crumpled to the floor in shock. "How could this happen?"

"You know how it is," Mae Lin said. "The

Flower Fairy was Ann's baby. She put everything into it. It's been in a slump for a while, but I didn't know it was that bad. Nobody did. She left a note saying she couldn't figure out how to get it back on track. She lost hope. She thought she'd never succeed. She gave up."

Zuri felt the room spinning.

What if she had placed an order with the Flower Fairy as soon as she arrived in VainGlory? Could that have helped Ann? Would it have given her enough hope to hang on?

A pang of guilt sickened Zuri.

She knew what it felt like to lose hope. To convince herself that she'd become worthless and that her existence was pointless. She recalled the terrible sensation of feeling as if she'd tumbled off a cliff, plummeting down and down and down. The numbness. The sensation of not belonging in a world that seemed as if it had been made for everyone else except Zuri. The isolation that made her feel like the lowest being on the planet. And the inevitable conclusion that she didn't matter, couldn't matter, had no ability to make herself matter.

But since the beginning of their friendship, Zuri and Mae Lin had made a pact: whenever one of them slipped, she would tell the other. When Zuri sank into hopelessness, she told Mae Lin, who would plunge into the iciness of Zuri's despair and pull her back to the surface of confidence like a lifeguard rescuing and then resuscitating a drowned victim.

And Zuri did the same for Mae Lin. Together, they felt invincible.

Zuri pushed back the Flower Fairy icon and put Mae Lin's image front and center. "I'll bring you to VainGlory as soon as I can. I promise you'll be here soon. And then the rest of our lives will be perfect."

Mae Lin sniffed. "I know. I wish I could have helped Ann."

Zuri's heart felt like an anchor. "Me, too."

"Aspire is a wonderful place," Mae Lin said. "But sometimes it's hard. And I don't know how to help everybody. I don't know how to know when they need help. If I knew, maybe I could do something."

"Maybe we can figure it out someday," Zuri said, meaning it. "But right now, we have each other, and the most important thing is for me to bring you to VainGlory. You'll be safe here. We'll both be safe. And once we have our own lives in order, we can think about how to help other people in Aspire."

Mae Lin nodded. "OK."

But her voice sounded tired and worn down.

Zuri worried. "You have to call me if you feel bad. That's the deal."

"I know." Mae Lin offered a sad smile. "I will. It's just losing Ann. I found out a couple of minutes before you called. Everybody has their ups and downs, but I thought Ann would turn things around. I never dreamed she'd give up. It's hard."

"Yeah. It's hard for me, too." Zuri hesitated. She'd called Mae Lin for a reason, and she felt an urgency while at the same time not wanting to dismiss the death of their friend. "But we always say the best thing is to stay focused on our work."

"Right." Mae Lin straightened her posture and wiped away her tears. "You called for a reason."

"Remember how we got our first break?"

"That was a long time ago."

"I'm going to do the same thing here in VainGlory, and I need what we used back then."

Mae Lin paused in thought. "What we have now is better. I can make some updates and send them to you in a few days. Is that soon enough?"

"It's perfect. And don't forget. Call me anytime you need."

Mae Lin nodded before disconnecting.

Her icon diminished back into the wall, which became lively as more icons woke up in preparation for the upcoming day. Hundreds of icons buzzed in conversation and movement meant to catch Zuri's eye. She stared mindlessly at them. Her Personal

Soundtrack played an upbeat tune, and the vocalists sang about a new restaurant opening tonight. "Order now," they crooned, "and we'll deliver tonight! You won't have to think about it later!"

Zuri's stomach rumbled. Without thinking, she called up the singing icon and placed her order.

"Zuri!" Benjamin said.

As if startled out of a dream, she turned to see his image still sat on the sofa next to her.

"What are you doing?" he said.

Zuri pointed at the icon that now sank back to its place on the wall. "Dinner. If I order it now, I won't have to think about it later."

"One of your friends killed herself. How are you feeling?"

For a moment, Zuri missed the old Benjamin and his bright and persistent optimism. While it could sometimes be annoying, Zuri knew she needed someone like him to help her stay focused and assured. She assumed he'd either received an automatic upgrade or was programmed to adapt to her personality.

But with Mae Lin in Aspire, Zuri also liked having someone to lean on here in VainGlory, even if that someone ultimately was made of nothing but ones and zeroes.

"Not great," Zuri admitted. "Nothing feels very real at the moment."

"It there anything I can do to help?"

"I don't know."

"Mae Lin seems like a good friend. I'm glad you have her."

Zuri let out a sigh of relief. "Me, too. If it wasn't for Mae Lin, I could have been like Ann years ago. No one ever tells you how hard it is just to exist."

"Do you think it could help to have more people like Mae Lin in your life?"

"More people," Zuri murmured. Her mind buzzed with the germ of a new idea. She looked into Benjamin's eyes, which now appeared to pulse slightly. "That's the answer. What if I found a new best friend here in VainGlory? Maybe even a boyfriend."

"What about Mae Lin?"

Zuri waved a hand as if brushing away Benjamin's question. "Mae Lin will always be my actual best friend. I'm talking about finding friends who can help me get endorsements. Powerful friends. Ones who can help me get clusters and breaking trends."

The light in Benjamin's eyes pulsed faster. "But then you'd be using them."

"Not really," Zuri said. "I'm going to find people I truly like. And if I can help them in return, I'll do it. But what I need is to find the most powerful people who want to be seen with a rising star in VainGlory."

When Benjamin said nothing in response, Zuri added, "That's me. I'm on the verge of becoming a rising star, and with help from a few new best friends, I can do it."

CHAPTER 9

For the next few days, Zuri spent every waking moment scouring the icons inside her Personal Bubble. After realizing most were sites she'd used when living in Aspire, Zuri pushed them into the far background and tapped into the myriad of icons that catered to her new fellow residents. Most of those icons offered products and services beyond the financial reach of people who lived outside VainGlory.

Before beginning her hunt for new and influential friends, Zuri decided how to present herself to the world. She settled on wearing Mae Lin's bubble dress, where tiny bubbles floated randomly across the dress's black background, the bubbles changing constantly in a cycle from pale pink to lavender to burnt orange.

Every time Zuri brought up a new icon,

she examined the images of customers circling around it. She strained to hear each one, but they talked so loud and fast and all at once that it sounded more like a congregation of geese than people. When they changed their images to show how they used the product or service, Zuri hurried to comment in an effort to catch their attention.

But everyone appeared so absorbed in what they had to say that they didn't notice her.

It had been like that in her early days in Aspire. Zuri knew the solution to the problem was persistence. If she kept trying different icons and every person circling each icon, Zuri would succeed sooner or later.

Late in the day at the end of the week, Zuri slumped in exhaustion. Once again, she'd forgotten to eat dinner, but she felt no hunger while trudging forward. She struggled to keep her eyes open.

One more. I'll check just one more and then go to bed.

Her Personal Soundtrack played a soothing but perky number, which helped Zuri stay awake.

She'd already scoured the most popular sites for shopping and self-pampering. After navigating to the overview level of sites targeted to VainGlory residents, Zuri decided to try the category dedicated to fun.

New icons flooded her bubble wall, and the dissonance of yammering and music from those sites and their customers drowned out Zuri's Personal Soundtrack. Bright white searchlights emerged from one icon and swept across the depth and breadth of her wall.

Intrigued, Zuri brought forward the icon with the searchlights. Across the icon's top border, neon lights announced:

LookAtMeDance!

Unlike any other site she'd seen, the icon appeared as an empty dance floor, but music poured out of it. Hundreds of customer bubbles floated around the empty dance floor, each containing a single dancer, a pair of dancers, or a group, all responding to the music in their own way. In one bubble, a little girl appeared as a kitten wearing a tutu and performed clumsy pirouettes. As required by law, her age displayed below her spinning feet along with a padlock preventing adults from approaching her. In another bubble, a pair of men sporting cubist shapes humped in time to the music. In a larger bubble, several photorealistic women wearing sleek cocktail dresses formed a chorus line, where the one in the center wore a headdress reading "Bride to Be."

Zuri wilted. It could take hours to comment on everyone. But if she worked her way through them methodically, she could mark this off her task list and eventually go to bed.

After a few dozen failures, a woman dressed like a warrior in ancient Rome caught Zuri's attention. Dancing with energetic abandon, the woman presented as an anime figure with straight hair falling in sheets and huge round eyes that never blinked.

As she'd done with the others, Zuri projected a sphere containing her own image near the Roman warrior's presence. Shouting above the music, Zuri said, "Wow! I like the way you dance!" A smiling mouth floating out of Zuri's sphere and piled on top of the others beneath the warrior.

She kept dancing but pointed at Zuri. "Hey," the woman shouted. "I know you. I know that dress. Are you the one who punched the shark?"

Zuri came fully awake in an instant, forgetting to be tired. "Yes! That's me."

The woman spun and then conjured up an Invite button that hovered by her hand. "Meet me in the Talk Room."

For the first time Zuri realized the empty dance floor in the icon was replicated for every dancer. That dance floor dropped open beneath the warrior woman's feet, and she plummeted out of sight.

However, the Invite button still hovered, now in empty air.

Zuri hesitated, considering her options.

I don't know this woman. She's a stranger. Why is she so eager to talk to me when no one else is?

The thought of turning off the display of icons on her bubble wall and going to bed tempted Zuri.

But isn't that exactly the kind of friend I'm looking for? Even if we don't become friends, she might introduce me to someone else who will become my friend.

Zuri remembered how shy she'd felt when she first arrived in Aspire. It had taken months for her to work up the courage to approach fans of other sites. Even now, she still felt shy.

It's not like I have to talk to her in person. I'm in the safety of my Personal Bubble. Nothing bad can happen to me here.

Zuri jabbed at the Invite button before she lost her nerve.

Immediately, the image of the interior of a marble temple encircled by soaring fluted columns filled Zuri's Personal Bubble. Red banners hung among the columns, filling the space between them. The anime woman walked to stand face to face with Zuri. "Hi, I'm Milan. I'm a Blue-Blood VainGlorian. Do you know what that is?"

"No," Zuri said. Her empty stomach churned again, and her body felt like a hollow pit. "Does that mean you're royalty?"

Milan laughed. "In a sense. It means I'm native. Born and bred in VainGlory." She raised her chin slightly. "Sixth generation. My great-great-great grandparents were among the original founders of this city."

Zuri's heart raced. If she could get an endorsement from Milan, it could spiral into clusters and breaking trends.

Milan had the power to change Zuri's life.

Milan cocked her head to one side. "Is that really how you want to present yourself to VainGlory? You're not a kid, are you?"

Startled, Zuri didn't know how to answer at first. Finally, she said, "No. Do you think I look like one?"

Milan walked in a circle around Zuri, the background of the temple adjusting to her stride. "It's gauche to present your real face in VainGlory."

"Are you saying I should make my appearance look like a cartoon?"

"No one uses cartoons anymore."

"But you look like a cartoon."

Milan smirked. "Anime. It's different. Cartoons are for the unsophisticated."

"But my supervisor presents as a cartoon. She looks like a caterpillar."

Milan raised an eyebrow. "Oh, that's a strategy. Your boss wants to lull you into a sense of complacency. No one feels threatened by a cartoon caterpillar."

Zuri didn't know whether to believe Milan or not. She argued without thinking.

"But there's a little girl dancing who looks like a kitten."

Milan examined Zuri's appearance. "My point exactly. Little girls make themselves look like cartoons. Grownups don't." She spread her hands apart and used them to frame Zuri. "The Impressionist look might suit you. Or the poster type from the Moulin Rouge. The ones done by Toulouse-Lautrec. You know, his posters of the stars of Paris."

Zuri brightened. "That's perfect." She imagined how wearing Mae Lin's dresses and displaying them in that form could make them shine and capture the imaginations of VainGlorians.

Milan rocked a step back to ponder the thought. "I can help you put it together. If you like, we could even bring up a canal behind you and have a shark jump out of it. The shark would have that poster vibe, too, so everyone will know it's not real. It's a way to remind them who you are and what you've done."

Zuri hesitated. "I don't know if I want people to think of a shark every time they see me. It's not what I'm about."

Milan gave a thoughtful nod. "We could put it on a random loop. Experiment with the timing. Try having it come into view once an hour or once a day. It wouldn't brand you. It wouldn't define you. It would be a once-in-awhile reminder."

"I suppose."

"Good!" Milan smiled and rubbed her hands together. "Let's get started, Zuri."

Zuri recognized an opportunity when she saw one. She could have spent weeks or months trying to get the attention of a true VainGlorian. The reluctance she'd felt when Milan had first invited her to this Talk Room vanished. Zuri trembled with excitement, trying not to show it.

Milan's offer to revamp Zuri's online appearance promised to be the beginning of the kind of friendship that Zuri needed.

It wasn't until after they'd spent hours together and planned to meet the next day that Zuri struggled to remember whether or not she had told Milan her name—or if Milan had remembered it from seeing the shark attack.

CHAPTER 10

The next morning, Zuri woke up to the dim light of her Personal Bubble with its wall of icons muted and trembling for attention. She kept them that way until having dressed for the day, even though everyone connected to her would see the new Toulouse-Lautrec image that Zuri projected of herself. Following Milan's advice, Zuri adjusted her image to continue wearing Mae Lin's bubble dress but in another altered form. Today, she commanded the dress broadly outlined in the style of Toulouse-Lautrec to transform into knickers and a vest. Touting the artist's style of bold shapes and solid colors, the outfit appeared solid black with bright red bubbles drifting up and down the legs of the knickers, while letting the vest shift between solid black and solid red.

After ordering breakfast and picking it up from the delivery cube built into her wall, Zuri sat down on her living room sofa to eat her croissant, fresh from a local bakery. She brought the icons forward, removing the mute.

The onslaught of noise from the hundreds of icons made her wince. When she lived in Aspire, Zuri could rarely bring up more than a few sites at once because of her Slim Goggles' limitations.

Now inside her own Personal Bubble, the icons seemed infinite. Zuri wondered if she'd ever get used to the noise.

Her Personal Soundtrack kicked in, eas-ing ominous music over the disharmony of the icons.

Responding to the music, Zuri tensed, even though she sensed no reason to be alarmed.

Although she'd done nothing to approve it, the icon of an owl with a letter-size envelope clutched in its beak flew front and center. Once the icon enlarged to the size of a door, framed with the words "Incoming Message," the owl dropped the envelope at Zuri's feet and flew away.

Zuri's name appeared in large block letters on the envelope. A bright blue button materialized under her name. The words "Press Here" flashed inside the button.

Cellos and violins, supported by the heartbeat of a drum, played music in a minor chord. Zuri took it as a warning.

But when she tried to dismiss the Incoming Message, Zuri couldn't force herself to do it.

Instead, she reached down with one fingertip and pressed the button.

The envelope opened itself, and a realistic visual of Karen stood in front of Zuri. "By the time you get this," Karen's image said, "I'll be gone."

Startled to see the woman who had tried to upstage her, Zuri clutched her croissant before she could drop it, causing it to shed flakes on her lap. Zuri couldn't imagine what Karen wanted or why she would have any reason to contact her.

Karen pointed to her bandaged arm. "First, thanks for this." She paused and then corrected herself. "I mean, you saved my life. That shark would have killed me. The doctors say I'm alive because of you."

Zuri softened. She knew this was a prerecorded message, not a live conversation. Even so, Zuri whispered, "You're welcome."

Karen's message continued. "We're from different places that aren't so different. You're from Aspire, I'm from Ascend. We both know what it's like to start with nothing and build a life. And getting to VainGlory makes us the cream of the crop."

Zuri felt the butter from the croissant, slick on her fingers. Her stomach growled. She didn't want to take her eyes from

Karen's face but she didn't want to take another bite of the croissant without watching for flakes crumbling off its surface. Enough had already fallen.

"Look." Karen looked at Zuri directly, and her voice held no nonsense. "This is what everybody wants. To make it to VainGlory. To get rich and famous." Karen's voice lowered to a whisper that Zuri had to strain to understand. "But there's something wrong here. A shark attacks me in the middle of a park? When we're at a show that's meant to introduce us to the elite that we hope will become our customers?" Karen shook her head. "This can't be right."

Zuri's mind raced. Everything had been explained to her. Sharks lived in the waters surrounding VainGlory. One finding its way into the city had been a glitch.

Just a glitch.

Karen kept her voice to a whisper. "I know they say fame is the name of the game, but it's not worth dying for." She appeared to search Zuri's eyes. "Is it?"

Before Zuri could think of a response, Karen spoke in her normal voice again. "Because you helped me, I thought you should know that you have one less competitor. I'm going back to Ascend. I'd rather be a big fish in a small pond than shark bait in VainGlory." The recorded image of Karen searched Zuri's eyes once more. "Maybe you'd like that, too. Think about it."

The image of Karen folded up until it reduced to the size of a letter and stuffed itself back in the envelope.

That envelope burst into flames and quickly smoldered into ashes. The cartoon figure of a faceless maid stepped into the frame of the Incoming Message icon and swept the ashes up with a small handheld vacuum cleaner. Without further ado, the large doorway of the icon condensed back to its small size and returned to the wall of icons.

Zuri returned her attention to the croissant in her hands, startled to see that she'd gripped it so tightly that flakes now covered her lap, the sofa, and the floor below.

CHAPTER 11

"Zuri?" Benjamin materialized next to her on the sofa after Zuri finished her breakfast and cleaned up the mess made by the croissant.

Despite knowing that Benjamin was nothing more than a program built into her Personal Bubble, Zuri realized she was growing fond of him. Most interruptions annoyed her, but she didn't mind it when Benjamin popped into view. "Hey, Ben. What's up?"

A gray cloud fell over the wall of icons, blocking them from view. At the bottom of the cloud blinked the words "Privacy Wall."

Zuri pointed at it. "What is that? What did you do?"

"It blocks out the rest of the world. No one can hear us."

Feeling disconnected made Zuri distraught. "I don't understand. Why would anyone want to do that?"

"I heard what Karen said." His pale green eyes blinked but his metallic face held no expression, as usual.

Zuri forced what she intended to be an amused laugh, but it sounded strained and forced to her ears. "Yeah? So?"

"I'm supposed to give you advice when I see a need for it," Benjamin said. "I see a need for it."

Zuri turned to him in surprise. "Now? Why?"

She would have sworn she heard him sigh with worry.

"You're an artist," Benjamin said. "Like a painter or a musician or a dancer. There's one thing all artists have in common: passion and purpose."

"That's two things."

The hue of Benjamin's eyes intensified. "Technically, yes. But they boil down to the same thing. Karen may not have stated her passion and purpose, but she made a decision based on them."

"I don't think so. I think she's spooked. If they'll let her, I bet she comes back next week."

"Zuri, the world isn't always as it seems, especially here in VainGlory. The one thing that can keep you on course is passion and purpose."

"Still two things." Zuri fidgeted. She

tried waving her hands to dismiss the Privacy Wall, but the gray cloud remained in place.

"Why are you a designer?" Benjamin said.

Frustrated with him, Zuri made no attempt to prevent the edge in her voice when she answered. "You already know why. Everybody in VainGlory wants the same thing. Fame is the name of the game."

"You want to be famous? Why?"

Zuri tried punching the gray wall and then kicking at it, all to no avail. "Because I want to be happy."

"You think being famous will make you happy?"

Zuri rolled her eyes. "Have you ever seen anyone rich and famous who isn't happy?"

"Yes."

Zuri's tone darkened. "What do you know? You're not real. You don't know what it's like to be alive. You don't have to worry about being unhappy." She pointed at the gray cloud. "Do something! Get rid of this."

A wall of photographs emerged from the cloud.

One photograph showed Zuri as a giggling child, holding a puppy. Others displayed her family. More showed Zuri and Mae Lin together in Aspire.

The sight of the photos disgusted Zuri.

In every picture, she saw failure. The failure to get noticed. The failure to achieve. The failure to be connected to a world that needed to love her.

"Get rid of those," Zuri said, feeling more hostile by the moment. "Delete them. I never want to see them again."

A beam of light cut through the gray cloud, and an icon from the wall behind it burst forward. Before Zuri could react, Benjamin and the photographs faded away, while the Incoming Connect icon opened up into a large doorway. Milan appeared inside it, leaning against the doorframe. "Have you heard the news?"

Startled by Milan's unexpected arrival, Zuri didn't know what to say. She felt small in Milan's presence. Knowing that Milan was a VainGlory native, Zuri could only guess at her new friend's wealth and prestige. By comparison, Zuri felt like a nobody.

Milan snapped her fingers, and a book-size icon materialized in her hand. "That woman you saved? She left VainGlory. And her sales are going through the roof!"

"Karen?" Zuri remembered Karen's warning but didn't feel right sharing it with anyone. Karen's message had been for Zuri, not the entire world. If Karen had wanted to make a public announcement, that's what she would have done. Zuri was sure of it.

"Whatever," Milan said. With a flick of

her wrist, she pulled dozens of fan bubbles out of Karen's site, each filled with someone talking and gesturing. "Look at what people are saying."

As always, the voices talked over each other and were so loud that Zuri couldn't pick any words apart. "I can't understand any of them."

Milan flicked her wrist again and said, "One at a time."

A bright white light illuminated a fan bubble containing a woman wrapped in a towel and drying her hair. "Karen, don't go! We hardly knew you. Give me that dress you wore when the shark attacked you." The towel-wrapped woman raised her hand forward, and a green light glowed on the fleshy skin between her thumb and forefinger.

Zuri recognized the glow of the woman's implanted identity chip. Most people stored their money on their chips. Here, the toweled woman used hers to pay for Karen's dress.

The light left her bubble and lit up the one below hers, where a matron sat in an antique chair and sipped from a china cup. "Honestly, young lady. There's no need to give up so soon. Find your fortitude." She raised her hand, and it glowed green. "I'll have one of each from your collection."

The light shifted again, brightening an adjacent bubble of a bald man sporting a black goatee streaked with white. He seemed to be naked in bed with the sheets gathered around his waist. A dozing woman sprawled next to him. He spoke in a hushed voice. "My wife bet you'd be the winner of this year's new crop of designers. She'll be disappointed when she finds out you're leaving. I'll take the first dress you wore." When he raised his hand and it glowed green, he amended, "Make that in my wife's size, not mine."

Baffled, Zuri said, "What is this?"

Milan offered a blank look. "Karen's fans. They're upset she's gone. They're buying up her stock while it's available. Once she goes back to HayTown or Cornville or wherever it is she comes from, her goods will be shunned by VainGlory." Milan rolled her eyes. "There's not much tolerance for quitters." Milan paused and reconsidered. "Well, except for whatever fan base you manage to acquire before you quit. But I don't advise it!"

Zuri couldn't help but remember Karen's warning.

There's something wrong here.

Milan's voice took an alarmed edge. "Zuri, tell me you're not thinking of quitting!"

"No," Zuri said, but even she wasn't convinced by the hesitation in her own voice.

"Please, Zuri," Milan said. "I need you."

Startled, Zuri stared at her in disbelief. "But you have everything. Why do you need me?"

Milan wrung her hands. "Think of it. There's one thing every native VainGlorian wants: to discover the next big thing. Usually, it's a new artist—a musician, a dancer, a singer—or a designer. I think you've got the potential to become the next big thing. If I'm the one who discovers you, that makes me the darling of VainGlory. I'll do anything to help you. So, please stay. Please."

Milan's revelation surprised Zuri but also made her feel the greatest hope she'd experienced since the day of learning she'd been accepted to VainGlory. "I'll stay."

Milan clapped her hands together in triumph. "Wonderful! Come inside and we'll start planning."

"What do you mean? Come inside where? And how?"

"Silly goose." Milan laughed. "There's so much about VainGlory you haven't seen yet." She gestured for Zuri to follow as Milan exited the doorframe of the Incoming Connect icon and vanished. Her voice drifted faintly. "Follow me."

Dumbfounded, Zuri looked around for her Personal Digital Assistant, seeing him nowhere. "Benjamin!" she whispered. "Where are you? I need help."

Zuri remained alone, staring at the

empty doorframe of Incoming Connect. Not knowing what else to do, she stood and walked toward it.

As she walked, the doorway eluded her, seeming to back away.

"Ow!" Zuri said when she walked into her living room wall, so focused on the doorway that she didn't notice the walls of her home in the faint background of her Personal Bubble.

"Not that way," Milan's distant voice called out. "Use your mind. Think about where you want to go, and you'll go there."

Zuri rubbed her forehead where the wall had banged into it. With outstretched arms, she felt her way back to her sofa, not wanting to change her vision inside her Personal Bubble. When she recognized the fabric of the sofa by touch, Zuri wrangled her body to sit on it. She then gave all her attention to the empty doorframe.

I want to follow Milan through that door. I'm walking to follow her.

Although Zuri's body remained seated on the sofa, the empty doorway now approached her, as if she were walking through it.

I'm doing it!

Zuri's excitement derailed her, and the doorway receded as if an earthquake had misplaced it.

That didn't deter Zuri. She thought about how she had succeeded and repeated those thoughts.

This time, Zuri felt as if she breezed through the open doorway, greeted by bright light inside the living room of an apartment with an adjacent hallway that stretched for blocks. The white alabaster walls and polished marble floors gleamed in the light, which poured in from a bank of French doors lining the living room and separating it from a golden balcony. Trees potted in elaborate vases created the sense of a garden setting. Elegant furniture formed sitting areas throughout the room, each area centered below a crystal chandelier.

"Good girl, you figured it out," Milan said. She stood in front of a granite fireplace and a large mirror framed in carved and gilded wood. "Welcome to my home."

CHAPTER 12

Zuri stared at the majesty of Milan's apartment, thinking no palace in the world could look more beautiful. She shivered in delight. "Are all the floors in the Platinum Tower like this?"

Milan raised an eyebrow in astonishment. "Platinum? Why would any of the towers look like this?"

Tearing her gaze from the luxury surrounding her, Zuri looked at Milan. "This isn't the Platinum Tower?"

Milan laughed. "I'm a native, not a newcomer."

"Are we still in VainGlory?"

Milan laughed harder. "Come and take a look." She walked across the room to the French doors and walked outside on the golden balcony.

When Zuri joined her, the view took her

breath away.

"I live in Tall Ship. That's what the building is shaped like. We're on the hundredth floor."

Looking straight down, Zuri saw nothing but ocean. The edge of the city stood the equivalent of a few blocks away, lined with stone and marble buildings that twisted and turned like tree trunks shaped by wind over centuries. One looked like an ice cream cone that had landed upside down on a sidewalk. A bridge lined with towering columns led across one waterway to a round theater with a marquee announcing the current production in demure lights. Canals penetrated the city like veins. Zuri saw a maze of marinas that ringed the city, each filled with sleek boats.

"The flock of pelicans is over there." Milan pointed to the left.

At first, Zuri couldn't make out what she looked at, striking her as little more than configurations of long stretches of small and narrow beach islands filled with back-to-back houses so that every home faced the ocean. It took a while for her to see the pelicans.

Each "pelican" was an engineered island community. And there were pelicans for as far as Zuri could see, circling around the main island of VainGlory.

"This building—the Tall Ship—stands on its own foundation in the ocean. The Pelicans are island communities but still considered part of VainGlory."

"Everything is so beautiful," Zuri said. "If I lived here, I'd never leave home."

Milan gave a twisted smile. "Now you're getting the idea. Hardly any of us ever do."

"But the other morning I went to the water garden, and I saw lots of people there."

Milan snorted. "Probably the nouveau riche. Most of them are stars and don't know what to do with sudden wealth."

"Like, movie stars?"

"Sure. Movie stars, pop and rock stars, sports stars. Up-and-coming artists of all kinds." Milan winked. "Including designers, so take note of what your foolish peers are doing now so you don't make their mistakes."

Zuri didn't know how to respond. She didn't know what kind of mistakes Milan meant, and Zuri felt too intimidated to ask.

Instead, she simply nodded in agreement.

"Oh!" Milan said in a bright voice. "The good news is that you can take advantage of them."

"Take advantage?" Zuri said. She fidgeted. "I don't think I want to take advantage of anyone."

"Don't be ridiculous. Everyone takes advantage of each other in VainGlory." Milan swept her arm across the panorama of the city at their feet. "If you take advantage of them, you'll get everything you want."

Zuri shifted her weight from one foot to the other, suddenly unable to find a comfortable stance. "I don't know. It doesn't feel right."

"Don't be silly." Milan cast a casual glance at Zuri and then returned her gaze to the city. "Look at us. I'm using you to improve my status. And you're using me to boost your career. We both know what we want. We're willing to help each other get there. What's wrong with that?"

"Nothing, I guess." Still, Zuri felt something heavy in the pit of her stomach, even though everything Milan said made sense.

"Now," Milan said. "Let me show you what we do for fun." She led Zuri back inside her lavish home, closing the balcony doors behind them. "Share mode," Milan announced in a loud voice.

A hummingbird made of precious stones zoomed in front of Milan, sparkling in the bright light. "Yes, Mistress," the hummingbird said in a high-pitched voice. It swept around the perimeter of the room and then hovered in front of Zuri. "Share mode complete," the hummingbird said.

An explosion of light rocked Zuri back on her heels. In a panic, she reached out to steady herself, startled by the rough texture that she recognized from her own sofa.

I'm home, not with Milan. This is just an illusion. I'm sitting down on my own sofa. I'm safe at home.

When the explosion of light faded away, Zuri recognized the surroundings of Milan's home in the background but saw a more refined wall of icons displayed in front of her. Instead of hundreds of everyday icons, she saw a few dozen that looked like elegant shop store windows, dressed to perfection.

Milan appeared next to Zuri. "I'm sharing my Personal Bubble with you," Milan said. She pointed to one shop window displaying tarts, eclairs, napoleons, and other pastries against a back-drop of Paris. "I have a weakness for French patisseries."

The shop window to its right contained diamonds falling like musical raindrops onto a field of porcelain violets. "And jewelry," Milan added.

Another shop window showed expensive stiletto shoes walking on their own volition down a miniature marble staircase. Milan released a wistful sigh. "And, of course, shoes."

When she clapped a friendly hand on Zuri's shoulder, Zuri jumped in surprise.

Wide-eyed with wonder, Zuri said, "This feels so real. How is it possible?"

Milan shrugged. "They say it's mostly the power of suggestion. But that's not why you're here. I want to show you what's possible. Let's decide how I can get you on a fast track."

"With a shop window like these?"

"You can't afford one. Not yet. This is what you want in the end. The trick is determining how to get you there from the lowly status you have now. But this is just one slice of my mosaic."

The term surprised

Zuri so much that she spoke before she could think better of it. "Mosaic? What does that mean?" As soon as the words fell out of her mouth, Zuri wished she could take them back, terrified of looking foolish and stupid in front of Milan.

"They haven't explained it to you yet? I'm surprised." Although she spoke with a feather-light tone, Milan failed to hide her condescending air. "This is part of my mosaic, which is everything I buy. Everything I want. Everything I consider. Each individual thing is like a tile in a mosaic. Everyone has hundreds of thousands of tiles in their mosaic. My mosaic is who I am. Without it, I'd be nothing."

Zuri decided it was better to risk appearing stupid with someone committed to helping her than anyone else. She drew up the courage to speak again. "Every Vain-Glorian has a mosaic? Does that mean I'll get one, too, when I make it to the Platinum Tower?"

Milan failed to contain her laughter. "Silly goose! You already have one!"

The weight in Zuri's stomach reeled. "How? When they gave me my Personal Bubble?"

Milan's laughter faded. "No, you've had it much longer than that. Your mosaic was created when you were a child, as soon as you were old enough to make your own choices. It's been growing ever since."

Zuri forgot her fear of looking ignorant. She needed to understand what her new friend was talking about. "How is that possible? No one told me about it." She racked her brain. "Who made my mosaic?"

Milan gestured to the curved wall of the Personal Bubble surrounding them. "The world. Every time you make a decision—what to eat, how to spend your leisure time, every business decision you make—it's recorded. For example, when you order food, everything you order is recorded by the restaurant. If you walk in a park, the surveillance cameras take note. When you purchase whatever you need to make designer clothing, the people who sell to you keep records."

"But that's a lot of different places." Zuri chewed on her lower lip in distress. "How does all of that end up in a mosaic?"

"They sell it," Milan said. She shrugged. "And sooner or later it ends up in one place. You'll be doing the same thing when you get to the Platinum Tower."

Startled, Zuri said, "I'll be doing what?"

"Selling information about your customers, of course. And that information will go into their mosaics. And then you'll use their mosaics to determine who your best potential customers are."

Manipulation. That's what Milan is talking about. She's telling me that I'll manipulate people into buying my work.

And that I've been manipulated all my life by people doing the same thing to me.

Horrified by Milan's words, the weight in Zuri's stomach became so heavy that she struggled to keep her balance and remain standing.

CHAPTER 13

"That's like an analysis or some kind of report," Zuri said. "You're telling me that my mosaic is really a breakdown of who I am."

"It works differently, but ... oh!" Milan said in an excited voice. "That gives me an idea! You should see what's new and electrifying in VainGlory right now. It could give us ideas."

While Milan directed her bejeweled hummingbird Personal Digital Assistant to change the display of the bubble wall, Zuri considered mosaics and tiles.

Could it be all that bad? What does it matter if anyone else knows I like to eat croissants for breakfast? Doesn't that mean bakeries can compete for my attention? What's wrong with that? Milan likes bakeries. So do I. How can there be a problem with having a mosaic?

Her stomach rumbled.

Instead of appearing as a veil allowing the background of Milan's home to show through, the wall of the Personal Bubble they shared blackened. The shop windows vanished, replaced by framed images that looked like book covers or movie posters. Slowly and deliberately, they rotated on a carousel. When each one stopped before the women, it came forward and dominated their vision. The first showed a boisterous gathering of VainGlorians on a rooftop, where the city glittered against the night sky. White fog poured from their mouths.

Milan nudged Zuri and said, "Forget that one. Opium is fun when you have nothing to lose, but you're not ready for that yet."

The next image to come forward revealed a catwalk where muscular young men wearing little more than hats and thongs strutted for approval. When a redhead came to the end of the runway, he winked at Zuri.

"Again," Milan said, "maybe later but not for now."

Zuri avoided making eye contact with the redhead when he looked back over his shoulder at her, walking away as the catwalk image retreated and moved on.

Screams permeated the air when the next image jumped toward them, so dark that it exposed nothing until enough light faded to show a young woman dead on a floor.

Zuri cringed. She covered her eyes with one hand and clung to Milan with the other.

"This is what I want you to see," Milan said. "When you talked about analysis, you gave me the idea. Take a look."

Zuri peeked through her fingers to see uniformed police and men in dark suits circle around the body. A ticker ran below the image, reading *Can You Solve the Crime Before They Do?*

"Everyone loves a good mystery," Milan said. "It's even better when it's real. We get a steady feed from the violent cities. Some are real-time, but most are edited so they don't get boring."

Zuri didn't need anyone to explain the violent cities to her. She knew about the dozens of cities throughout the country where multiple murders happened daily. If not for her drive to create, she would have considered becoming a lawyer or detective.

The image of investigation and Milan's words chilled Zuri. It dawned on her that the VainGlorians depended on the suffering of others for entertainment.

Zuri remembered Karen's warning about something not being right in VainGlory. Could this be what she meant?

Zuri considered her last conversation with Mae Lin and wondered if her friend might be right about returning to Aspire and being content with the success they'd already accomplished in VainGlory.

Zuri thought about what Benjamin had said about passion and purpose before she'd interrupted him. Had her own Personal Digital Assistant been on the verge of advising her to return to Aspire and focus on her work instead of seeking fame and riches in VainGlory? Why would a program designed to help her succeed in VainGlory do such a thing?

"This is the tip of the iceberg," Milan said. She swiped the icon, and a news feed displayed. A suited man sat at a news desk and said in mid-announcement, "... reported missing today. Although expected to return to Ascend, her presence is silent on all sites, and those who attended her scheduled arrival claim they never saw her."

Zuri's misgivings heightened as she let her hand fall away from her face. "Karen? Are they talking about Karen?"

"Boring," Milan proclaimed as she swiped the news image out of sight.

"Please go back. I think they're talking about Karen. She's from Ascend."

"So are a lot of other wanna-be artists who come to VainGlory. They might be talking about someone else." Milan swiped through a few other news feeds. "I saw her going-away message. When people get kicked out of VainGlory, they're often so ashamed that they don't go through the correct channels and fill out the expected paperwork. It's impossible to leave the city without removing your Personal Bubble and leaving it behind, and many people don't find that out until they're at the border, ready to go. They remove their Personal Bubble and drop it, which leaves them with no way to connect to the world. It's a common mistake to think they've gone silent, when the problem is that it takes time in whatever city they arrive to acquire one of those sad little devices to replace their Personal Bubble."

"Slim Goggles," Zuri said. "We use Slim Goggles."

"Whatever." Milan shrugged. "My point is that people in Cornville or Haytown or wherever panic when the VainGlory reject doesn't seem to be there and report them missing. It happens all the time."

Milan's explanation sounded logical to Zuri. But for some reason she couldn't pinpoint, Zuri didn't like it.

The rotating icons halted and displayed an image of VainGlorians running through the Carnival of Animals park, screaming in a panic while masked people wielding bloody knives chased them.

"Wonderful!" Milan said. "This is the one I want you to see. It's last month's Murder Dash. I've run it so much that it does nothing for me anymore, but I know people who have done it for decades. The next one is coming up soon, and they're always looking for sponsors. If you become one, the attention will be massive."

Zuri took a closer look. Men and women dressed in high-end athletic gear raced through the park, sometimes using the crystal animals as obstacles or hiding behind them. No one appeared injured. "Does anyone get hurt?"

Milan guffawed. "Only the ones chasing them. It's all about the thrill of the chase."

In the park, a man crouching behind a crystal gorilla stood and touched its shoulder when a masked woman crept close.

The crystal gorilla swept the masked woman into its grasp and crushed her skull.

Zuri shrieked in horror.

The man who had hid behind the gorilla gave a shout of victory.

"Oh, don't feel bad for that one," Milan said. "The ones doing the chasing are real criminals."

"Murderers?" Zuri cried in dismay. "People want to be chased by real murderers?"

"No. Mostly, they're shoplifters or frauds. We don't tolerate that kind of criminal in VainGlory." Milan smirked. "Once they're convicted, they're offered a deal. If they can run the Murder Dash and get to the end, they're set free."

Zuri pieced everything she'd seen and heard together. "And the Carnival of Animals kills them?"

"Only when activated by a VainGlorian. You saw that man touch the gorilla's shoulder? That's the signal to take care of the closest criminal. The masks are fastened in place so they can't be removed. That's how the animal recognizes the target—by the mask."

What kind of city is this?

Zuri fidgeted, crossing her arms and then rubbing her hands against her face. Her fingers felt rough and dry, as if she were made of straw. Empty, hollow straw, brittle to the touch. Like the straw her hands had once brushed against when she was young and running through the corridors created by bales of straw in a maze.

For a moment, Zuri promised herself that when she left Milan's bubble and returned to her own that she'd make plans to go back to Aspire.

But then an old idea combined with a new idea, and she saw a way to live in VainGlory on her own terms.

CHAPTER 14

Later that day, Zuri left the bubble she had shared temporarily with Milan and returned to her own. She diminished her familiar wall of icons until she recognized the interior of her new home in the Gold Tower. For good measure, Zuri paced her living room in silence for a few minutes.

Whispering, she said, "Ben? Are you here?"

The image of the robot materialized in front of her, his eyes glowing pale green. "I'm here, Zuri. What do you need?"

Not knowing how he'd react, Zuri took a leap of faith. If she made the wrong decision now, her plan could be relayed to Donna, and Zuri doubted her supervisor would approve. She continued to whisper. "The Privacy Wall."

As she'd seen before, a gray cloud fell

over the wall of icons, blocking them from view. "Privacy Wall" blinked below it.

"No one can hear us?" Zuri said.

Benjamin nodded. "That's right."

"I need your help."

Benjamin leaned closer. "Tell me what you need."

Zuri decided it would make the most sense if she explained everything point by point so Benjamin could follow her logic. "When I lived in Aspire, the greatest success I had with Mae Lin was when we created an online maze."

Benjamin's green eyes wavered. "I don't understand."

"We challenged our customers to go through the maze. There were closed doors and overhead panels and trap doors. Behind most of them, there was nothing. But behind some of them, we put one of Mae Lin's designs. Whoever found it first won it. People loved the maze, and our sales were great. I want to do something like that here."

"And you want me to help you create a maze like that?"

"Yes. But a regular maze will be too boring for VainGlorians. They want excitement." The more Zuri thought through her idea, the more she liked it. "We'll have monsters chase them through the maze, and they'll have to look for doorways or other ways to get to safety. We'll put one of

Mae Lin's designs behind some of them—and each design will trigger a weapon that will destroy the monster. When the monster is a vampire, stakes will shoot out of the design and hit the vampire in the heart. When the monster is a were-wolf, we'll use silver bullets. We'll have all kinds of monsters and weapons. The VainGlorians will get the thrill of a chase, and they'll be surprised when Mae Lin's outfits make them feel like warriors."

"And your supervisor has approved this?"

Zuri glanced at the gray cloud of the Privacy Wall, still firmly in place. "No. I don't think she would approve. But I don't approve of how the VainGlorians use people. I don't like the way they manipulate or feel entertained by tragedy."

Benjamin tilted his head slightly to one side. "If you don't seek approval from your supervisor, are you not guilty of the same thing?"

"Maybe."

If Benjamin had been a real man standing in front of her, Zuri would have felt intimidated by her low status in VainGlory. She would have cowered and fell silent.

But she had no problem talking to a robot.

Zuri continued with passion. "I could go home to Aspire right now, but what good would that do? What if there's a chance to show VainGlorians that there's a better way? That they can get the thrills they want without hurting anyone?"

"It could be dangerous."

"I've thought about that." Zuri resumed her pacing. She'd been thinking about it all day. "The people in real danger appear to be criminals, and low-level ones at that. I'm not breaking any law. I'm not hurting anyone. I'm putting a new twist on promoting Mae Lin's work. That's all. And if VainGlorians like it, maybe fewer of them will do terrible things. Maybe they'll become better people."

"That's a tall order. I see no one else doing anything like that."

Zuri stopped and stared at Benjamin. "That's my point. If I go back to Aspire, I'm turning my back on something I might be able to change. People who live in murder cities don't deserve to be exploited. A shoplifter doesn't deserve to have her head crushed by a gorilla. How can I sleep now that I know what goes on here without trying to do something about it?"

For a moment, she thought the corner of Benjamin's metallic mouth lifted in a half-smile, but the next moment he looked normal. Zuri decided she must have imagined it. What reason would a program displayed as a robot have to smile?

"Would you like to start now?" Benjamin said.

CHAPTER 15

Keeping the Privacy Wall in place, Benjamin summoned forward the image of a small personal safe. He entered a sequence of numbers on the keypad.

A red light flashed on the door of the safe, and a blast of sound made Zuri cover her ears. "What's happening?" she said.

Benjamin took a step back and reconsidered the safe. "Someone changed the combination. It's typically set to the birthdate of the owner."

"Who's the owner?"

Benjamin looked at her. "You, of course. This space is reserved for your use."

"Then why is it locked?"

"The space is reserved for you and you alone. You're the only one who should access it, and that happens through me."

"Then how did the combination get changed?"

"Good question." Benjamin tried entering different combinations, but each resulted in a flashing red light and a blast of noise.

The gray cloud of the Privacy Wall quivered but held in place.

Zuri made several suggestions: Mae Lin's birthdate, the date Zuri arrived in Aspire, and the date she was accepted to VainGlory.

None worked.

Benjamin tried one more combination. This time, the light on the safe door turned green, and the door popped open. He turned toward Zuri and answered her question before she could ask it. "The date you arrived in VainGlory."

Zuri smiled as Benjamin manipulated the safe and enlarged it to fill her Personal Bubble.

The robotic man gestured for Zuri to follow him inside. "Illuminate," he said. Light filled the chamber, which appeared to extend into infinity.

The space reminded Zuri of the interior of a large air duct. The narrow walls allowed only two people to walk side by side, while the ceiling towered high above. Metallic echoes rang with every step they took.

"Is it possible to soften how it looks?" Zuri said. "It's a bit industrial."

Benjamin pressed one hand against the wall, and the appearance of the chamber changed.

Now, they walked on wooden floorboards that creaked with every step. Old-fashioned wallpaper filled with cabbage-like purple flowers peeled from the walls. Black-and-white photographs of people with stern expressions and 19th-century garb hung for as far as Zuri could see. Gleaming tin tiles pressed with diamond-shaped designs covered the ceiling.

Benjamin said, "If you want people to get chased by monsters through a maze, maybe it should feel like a haunted house."

Zuri clapped her hands together. "It's perfect."

As they walked through the long chamber, Zuri opened every door, every panel, every nook and cranny, to consider the best places to hide Mae Lin's designs for fans to discover and use to protect themselves from the monsters in pursuit.

She discovered one door locked, its knob refusing to turn when she twisted it. She spun to face her Personal Digital Assistant. "Ben? Why won't it open?"

"I don't know." Benjamin tried the knob, which didn't budge.

"If this space is for my use, why would any of it be off limits?"

"I don't know."

Zuri would have sworn that worry deepened Benjamin's voice. Suddenly concerned about being inside this space, she said, "Ben?"

Light from his pale green eyes beamed upon the door knob. He shut the beams off before looking at her. "Now, try it."

She glanced from Benjamin to the door and back again. "What did you do?"

"I made a suggestion to the door's programming. Try it. The door won't bite."

Standing as far away from the door as possible while still managing to grasp its knob, Zuri gave it one more attempt.

The door groaned as it swung open.

"Illuminate," Benjamin said to the room.

Soft white light cast down from the ceiling, even though Zuri saw no light fixture. The room stood empty except for a locked case in its center. The case looked like a steamer trunk that might have been carried onto the *Titanic*, covered with colorful travel labels from Paris, Rome, and London. Each end had a thick leather handle, and Zuri imagined it might weigh so much that two people had to carry it, one on either side. A heavy padlock kept the lid shut and inaccessible.

Benjamin walked with a purposeful stride into the room. Once he reached the steamer trunk, he looked back at Zuri. "You should see this."

The thought of going into the room

made Zuri's skin crawl, which had to be a good thing because it's how she wanted her fans to feel when being chased through this chamber.

It's just a room. Benjamin is right here. He's not going to let anything bad happen to me.

Zuri shook off her anxiety.

I'm being ridiculous. There's nothing to be afraid of.

When Zuri joined Benjamin's side, the first thing she noticed on the steamer trunk was the large label, addressed to Franklin Buckingham.

"Franklin Buckingham?" Zuri said, her trepidation giving way to confusion. Although Zuri had never owned anything grander than a pair of Slim Goggles for connecting to the world before coming to Vain-Glory, she knew all about the impressive technology the city had to offer and the man behind it. "He invented the Personal Bubble. He owns the company. What is a case addressed to him doing in a space that's supposed to be for me to use?"

"That doesn't worry me," Benjamin said. He pointed to finer print below the address. "This does."

That fine print consisted of one thing.

Zuri's name.

CHAPTER 16

The sight of Zuri's name on a case addressed to the most powerful man in Vain-Glory spun her into a new level of anxiety.

Karen's words haunted her.

There's something wrong here.

Zuri chewed on a fingernail. "How do you explain this?"

Benjamin's voice remained calm and even. "I can't."

This can't be right.

She shot a frightened glance at him. "Can you open it?"

Just as he'd done to change the appearance of the chamber, Benjamin placed his hand against the surface of the steamer trunk, which sizzled and popped at his touch.

Benjamin withdrew his metallic hand in a swift move. "The lock is more powerful than anything I've seen before."

I know they say fame is the name of the game, but it's not worth dying for.

Zuri paced. She waved her hands at her own face. "Do that mojo you did with your eyes to unlock the door."

Obeying, Benjamin cast beams of pale green light from his eyes.

The surface of the trunk crackled, extinguishing Ben's light. One end of each leather strap detached and unfurled, forming arms that stretched while the trunk made a yawning sound.

"Darken," Benjamin whispered to the room's ceiling.

Two fist-size cameras emerged from behind the case. Attached to thin metal rods, they looked like the wandering eyes of a crustacean.

The light in the room blinked out before the cameras could aim at Zuri and Benjamin.

Zuri bolted out of the room before Benjamin could suggest it. He followed close on her heels, shut the door, and beamed his gaze at the knob until the door locked back into place. "I wouldn't advise letting your fans into that room."

"I agree," Zuri said. "What was that? Did it see us? Does it know who we are?"

Benjamin's eyes paled so much that they seemed devoid of color for a moment. "Probably. With the light out inside the room, we were backlit. But considering this is your space, it limits the number of suspects."

"Suspects?" Zuri said in a panic. "We're suspects now?"

"Possibly. If someone asks, tell them the first thing you noticed on the label was your name, and you assumed it was meant for you."

"You think anyone will believe that?"

"Possibly. Tell them as soon as the case refused to open, you realized your mistake."

Zuri suppressed a shudder. She wished she were a skilled liar and worried that she'd never convince anyone of that story.

Although she'd been keeping her Personal Soundtrack at the lowest volume possible, she didn't mind when it increased in sound without her asking and played bright, happy music that melted her concerns away.

CHAPTER 17

After contacting Mae Lin and deciding which designs to use, Zuri directed Benjamin in their placement in the maze. Zuri then checked all the monsters he'd created and placed within the program of the maze, whose entrance now appeared as the façade of a haunted house.

Once Benjamin worked out the details of how each fan would enter and connect to the experience, Zuri tried to reach Mae Lin once more, unable to find her friend within her personal icon, their business icon, or at any of their favorite places.

Zuri stared at her wall of icons, humming along to the catchy tune played by her Personal Soundtrack. "Where are you, Mae Lin?" Turning to Benjamin, she said, "Can you find her?"

His pale green eyes deepened in color

for a moment. "I can't search Aspire. The Privacy Wall surrounding VainGlory won't let me out."

"Oh," Zuri said, unable to hide the frustration in her voice.

If Mae Lin lived in VainGlory, this wouldn't be a problem.

But remembering her new best friend, Zuri brought forward the Outgoing Connect icon from her wall. Moments later, Milan stepped into the icon's doorway.

"Zuri," Milan said in a sleepy voice. "Where have you been?"

"Working." A moment of panic and shyness seized Zuri, and her throat tightened. She focused on the fact that today Milan displayed as the murky figure that an Impressionist might have painted—not as her flesh-and-blood self, which Zuri had yet to see. The mere thought of looking at someone real made Zuri nervous, so she focused on the pretty colors and waviness of Milan's chosen shape.

"I've made something special," Zuri continued. "Something I think a lot of people in VainGlory will appreciate. I'm going to make the announcement on my business icon in five minutes. Would you please connect to it? I'd like to see you there."

"An announcement?" Milan's voice sounded suspicious. "It's been sanctioned?"

Her question posed an issue that Zuri didn't know how to answer. Zuri never had to have anything authorized or even approved when she lived in Aspire. Along with Mae Lin, the two women were free to do as they pleased when it came to spreading news about their work.

Zuri decided that if she pretended she hadn't heard Milan's question that Zuri wouldn't have to answer to any consequences.

"Thank you," Zuri said. "I'll see you soon." Before Milan could speak again, Zuri disconnected the icon and sent it back to the wall where it belonged.

Turning to Benjamin, Zuri said, "Let's go."

CHAPTER 18

Zuri gazed at the hundreds of icons on the wall surrounding her inside her Personal Bubble. She brought the icon for the business site she owned with Mae Lin forward, still frustrated at having no luck giving her friend a heads up about what would happen momentarily while at the same time believing it wouldn't be wise to wait. Zuri hoped Mae Lin would be pinged by her automatic notification of any change to their site and that her friend would understand.

For a moment, Zuri froze in terror.

What am I doing? What if I fail? I could ruin everything, not just for me but for Mae Lin.

Zuri took a deep breath to calm her nerves.

What if I do nothing? Hundreds of people

are invited to VainGlory every year and most go back home in weeks or even days. Look at Karen. She went back to Ascend the day she arrived in VainGlory. She didn't even last a day.

If I hesitate, I could lose Milan's friendship. Everyone knows how fickle Vain-Glorians are. I need to do something while I have her attention. She could forget about me and take up a new best friend tomorrow.

Zuri requested a Messenger. An array of animal images displayed: a snowy owl, a black-gloved fox, a velociraptor, and a winged horse. She dismissed the first two choices, because she worried they might be ignored.

Zuri beckoned for the velociraptor to step forward. It lunged for the horse's neck, but the other animal flew away without injury. The velociraptor turned its beady eyes toward Zuri. Its claws clacked against the floor as it walked toward her.

"Take this message to my friend," Zuri said, reminding herself that the dinosaur didn't exist, no matter how real it seemed. "Ask her to come to this icon at once."

The velociraptor snapped at Zuri, its teeth barely missing her hand. An envelope addressed to Milan materialized, impaled on its teeth. With a blood-curdling shriek, the velociraptor sprinted out of sight.

Benjamin emerged into view at the opposite end of Zuri's living room, standing inside the edge of her Personal Bubble. "Ready?"

Zuri gave him a quick glance. "Ready."

The icon of the business site she shared with Mae Lin came forward, and its outline glowed in bright lights to indicate its eagerness to broadcast Zuri's message.

A dozen bubbles surrounded the icon, showing the current visitors.

A new bubble popped into view, showing Milan sprawled on an elegant chaise lounge. She extended her hand and gave Zuri a thumbs up of approval.

"Welcome, everyone," Zuri announced to the small group of fans. "I'm here to announce something special."

Benjamin cleared his throat. Hearing him made Zuri realize she'd prepared with his help. No Personal Digital Assistant would steer his client wrong. She decided to trust his expertise.

She decided to trust her own, as well.

Zuri forced the best smile she could muster. "Tonight, six hours from now, I invite you to experience the first Monster Dash from me and my partner Mae Lin. You might know me for punching sharks. But after tonight, you'll be known for killing monsters."

A few dozen bubbles appeared around Milan's bubble, and each displayed one or more people marked with the VG label.

VainGlorians. They're all showing up

around Milan. They must be her friends. She's notifying her friends and telling them to watch me!

Gaining confidence, Zuri smiled without having to force it. "Tonight, step into our world."

As planned, the image of the haunted house she'd created with Benjamin appeared behind her.

"Come inside our haunted house, but beware! You won't know what kind of monster lurks around every corner."

Programmed by Benjamin for this moment, Zuri's Personal Soundtrack played spooky music, underlined by sounds of groaning floorboards and an occasional scream.

More friends popped up in bubbles surrounding Milan, and others showed up in her fan area.

The word is spreading. People are coming to hear what I have to say—and no one is leaving!

Fueled by this initial success, Zuri spoke with excitement. "You have every chance to escape the monsters. Look for doors on the walls around you. Look for hatches on the ceiling above. Look for trap doors beneath your feet."

The voices in the bubbles buzzed. Faces became animated with anticipation.

"Behind some of these places to hide," Zuri continued, "you'll find a design by Mae

Lin. Find it, and put it on to use as a weapon to kill the monster chasing you."

Dozens and then hundreds of bubbles containing VainGlorians filled Zuri's wall, blocking out the icons behind them. Everyone talked, and the buzz of their chatter became so loud that Zuri had to decrease her own bubble's volume.

"Best of all," she said, "when you succeed in killing a monster, the design you wear is yours. Everyone who uses one of Mae Lin's designs to kill a monster gets to keep that outfit. We're giving away 100 outfits tonight."

As planned, a "Join the Monster Dash" button appeared.

Immediately, clicks registered in Zuri's field of view, gaining the momentum of an avalanche.

More and more bubbles appeared, crowding against the ones already there.

The shout of hundreds of voices became so loud that Zuri said, "I'll answer every question, but I can't hear you. Please use the marquee to show your question."

A ticker scrolled at the bottom of the wall, and Zuri began reading questions out loud and answering them in a calm manner.

Inside, she wanted to jump up and down and yell in victory. Her eyes welled with tears, and she struggled to keep her composure.

It's finally happening. This is what I wanted. Mae Lin and I invested ten years and dreamed of this kind of success. It's real.

Zuri saw Milan wearing a wicked grin inside her bubble.

But no matter how much Zuri searched, she saw no sign of Mae Lin.

CHAPTER 19

After answering questions for a few hours, Zuri posted all her answers in a field next to the "Join the Monster Dash" button and disconnected from her site, ready to relax before tonight's event.

However, the Incoming Connect icon soon filled her space. Hoping it might be Mae Lin, Zuri answered.

Instead of Mae Lin, the image of a cocoon made of brown leaves, dry and brittle, appeared. Rustling sounds filled the air. The cocoon rolled toward Zuri, revealing an opening where she saw the face and upper body of a blue caterpillar, snug inside the cocoon.

Donna.

The sight gave Zuri optimism. "Did you see my announcement?"

"I did," the caterpillar said. "If you have

no interest in remaining in VainGlory, you should have simply told me and saved us all a lot of trouble."

If Donna had projected her human self instead of a cartoonish caterpillar, Zuri would have crumpled, incapable of speaking. As always, she found it easier to find the courage to speak to a cartoon than a person. Still, Zuri spoke in a voice raspy with shame. "I thought I was doing something good."

"I know. It's a rookie mistake. That's why I'm allowing you to stay, assuming you're willing to follow instruction."

Relief overwhelmed Zuri and washed away her shame. "Of course! Tell me what you want, and I'll do it."

"Good." Dozens of slender black arms on the caterpillar's upper body wriggled and reached out for a nearby green leaf. The arms passed the leaf up toward the insect's mouth, and the caterpillar took a healthy bite out of the leaf. When it spoke, green juice dribbled down its chin. "Of what value do you think you are to VainGlory?"

"Mae Lin's designs. She makes beautyful clothes that VainGlorians want to wear."

"Wrong." The caterpillar swallowed, oblivious to the green juice dripping across its face. "Your value comes from the information you can gather about your customers when they buy from you."

Zuri stared at the caterpillar, struggling

to understand.

"It isn't about you," Donna said. "It's about what you can do for VainGlory. And what VainGlory wants from you is data about your customers."

"That makes no sense," Zuri blurted. "Don't you already have all the data you need about your own citizens?"

The caterpillar stared at Zuri until the young woman shriveled. "Do you know what a mosaic is?" Donna said.

Zuri thought back to what Milan had told her about mosaics. "Everyone has a mo-saic. Everything someone buys or wants or considers is like a tile in a mosaic. Everyone has hundreds of thousands of tiles in their mosaic. That's why I don't understand why the city wants more."

"You always need more," the caterpillar said. "One person's tiles create a map of that person. A mosaic tells a story about who that person is. The more we know about who that person is, the better we can predict what products to create. What kinds of things to sell."

Zuri's optimism sank. "You never believed in me or Mae Lin. All VainGlory wants is to use us to get more tiles for every mosaic in the city."

"It's not as bad as that. Think of it this way. You and Mae Lin are designers, and VainGlorians love clothing. VainGlorians also have basic needs like food and furniture and entertainment. Through your art, the city can learn the best way to make its citizens happy." Donna's tone took a serious turn. "There are proven ways to succeed, but you have taken a turn in the wrong direction. I'm here to help you correct it."

The caterpillar used the leaf it chewed to wipe up the green spittle running down its face and then plastered the leaf against the exterior of the cocoon, covering some of its exposed legs. "You have four hours to improve your Monster Dash before it opens," Donna continued. "Make no mistake. If you fail to meet the minimum requirement for success, you will be escorted from VainGlory with no option to ever return. Consider this a life-or-death situation."

The caterpillar and the Incoming Connect icon diminished and sank back into the wall of icons.

"Wait!" Zuri cried out in a panic. "What am I supposed to do?"

A new icon took up the space in front of her. A neon sign reading Neural Network arched above an open doorway.

Assuming it must be the answer to her question, Zuri entered.

A casino sprawled around her, empty of customers but filled with rows of slot machines, and roulette, blackjack, and poker tables. Constant pings, bells, and shuffling sounds buffeted against her ears. The stench of alcohol and sweat permeated the air.

A slim slot machine with blinking red eyes rolled up to Zuri. "Good afternoon, Miss. Please follow me to your training session."

"Ben?" Zuri said.

The slot machine stopped blinking, appearing to stare at her in consternation. "No, Miss. I am assigned to you for today's training session only. If you prefer to refer to me by name, you may call me Isaac. Please. Follow me." Isaac rolled down one of the aisles flanked by lines of fellow slot machines, each one pinging in recognition as he passed by.

The purple carpet squished beneath her feet when Zuri walked behind him. Isaac zigged and zagged across the casino floor, finally settling on a small area containing only a single chair. Once Zuri entered that area, Isaac summoned up walls to surround it and block out the view of the rest of the casino. He extended his single slot arm toward the chair, gesturing for Zuri to sit down.

She took a cautious seat.

"I understand you have made many mistakes in your creation of a maze that will open soon," Isaac said in a matter-of-fact tone. "Today, you will learn how to correct those mistakes and keep from making any more like them in the future."

Frustrated because she didn't know what to expect, Zuri said, "Everyone makes mistakes."

Isaac's red eyes blinked slowly. "Of course. You are human. But recognizing when you've done something wrong is more important than recognizing when you've done something right. Learning to correct your course is what matters. It's how you learn and grow."

Zuri knew that, like Benjamin, Isaac was only a program. But his words made her feel understood. She wished she could embrace him, because he made her feel seen.

"Now," Isaac said, "let's begin. Pull my arm."

Zuri obeyed, reaching to grasp Isaac's single arm and pulling it down. After being extended toward the ground, his arm creaked back up to his shoulder.

His initial display showed an apple, a slice of pizza, and a brownie. Those images blurred out of sight, replaced by three spinning wheels, side by side. When the wheels stopped, the new display showed two images of the same shoe and a bracelet.

"Well done, Miss!" Isaac said. "You almost won on your first attempt. Try again."

Although it miffed Zuri that the machine appeared to be wasting precious time, she also felt a tug of excitement at nearly winning.

THE MOSAIC WOMAN

What if I win? Will that secure my place in VainGlory? Or does Isaac have the power to fix the problems for me? If I win, will I win his help?

Tempted to ask those questions out loud, Zuri bit her lip and moved his single arm again.

This time, two images of a gold bar labeled "100K" and one image of a silver bar labeled "50K" settled into place when the wheels stopped spinning.

"Even better!" Isaac said. "Miss, you have quite the knack for this game."

Zuri's misgivings slipped away, replaced by her focus on the slot machine. Mesmerized by what she could win, Zuri no longer needed Isaac's prompt to pull his arm. The sight of the three items displayed by every pull of the slot machine's arm drew her in closer.

One diamond bracelet and two squares that read "All Your Problems Solved."

Two images of the Platinum Tower and one image of a crystal unicorn wearing a necklace made of blue sapphires.

Three images of Mae Lin's bubble dress!

Zuri jumped to her feet in joy, only to sink back into her chair when the third image slowly turned one more space to reveal a pair of earrings.

"You can stop now," Isaac said.

"No," Zuri said, reaching for his arm. "I almost got it."

Isaac backed away from her. "I said, you can stop now."

Zuri pursued him. "I don't want to stop. Didn't you see how I almost won?"

Isaac eluded her. "This begins our lesson. Please return to your seat."

The desire to keep playing gnawed at Zuri like hunger. Attempting to quell that hunger, she remembered what Donna had told her.

You have four hours to improve your Monster Dash before it opens.

In that moment, Zuri didn't care about the Monster Dash. She didn't care about being in VainGlory or why she'd invested the last ten years of her life in striving to come here. She didn't care about her business, and she didn't care about Mae Lin.

She only cared about winning the game.

Make no mistake. If you fail to meet the minimum requirement for success, you will be escorted from VainGlory with no option to ever return. Consider this a life-or-death situation.

Remembering Donna's warning shocked Zuri out of her fugue. "What?"

Isaac pointed at the chair.

Zuri returned to it.

"Think about how you felt when you were playing my game," Isaac said.

Zuri couldn't help but stare at the three images displayed on his chest.

Isaac's red eyes followed her gaze. With a sweep of his single arm, he erased the three images, leaving the field where they had appeared blank.

Zuri's heart raced. The sense of disconnect from the game left her flustered and muddled. She looked into Isaac's eyes, hoping to persuade him. "Just one more?"

"Think about how you feel right now. Close your eyes. Concentrate. Identify your feelings."

Zuri didn't want to do anything Isaac suggested. All she wanted was one more try at slots, certain she stood on the verge of winning what she wanted. But she closed her eyes anyway.

Once more, she thought about Donna's words while taking Isaac's advice to identify her feelings.

Consider this a life-or-death situation.

Zuri chewed her fingernails, not knowing what else to do with her anxiety. If she failed now, then all the long years of hard work both she and Mae Lin had put in to achieve their place in VainGlory would be for nothing. Zuri thought about all the sacrifices they'd made.

It's our work that will bring us success. Not a slot machine.

She opened her eyes and looked at Isaac.

"Everything you experienced just now—everything you felt," Isaac said. "That's how you need to make your potential customers feel."

Zuri felt as if she'd just swallowed an ice cube. A terribly cold sensation ran down the back of her throat.

Isaac's red eyes stopped blinking. "And that's what you're here to learn."

CHAPTER 20

Despite her unease, Zuri became a quick study. For two hours, she followed Isaac's instruction about how to improve her Monster Dash. During the next two hours, she accepted his assistance in putting those instructions in place.

In the few minutes remaining before the event began, Zuri tried again to contact Mae Lin without luck. Their business icon displayed in Zuri's Personal Bubble alongside a countdown clock and a marquee sign reading "Monster Dash begins in..."

Zuri fidgeted on her living room sofa.

Mae Lin had held up her end of the bargain by delivering her latest designs for the Monster Dash. But where had she been since their last conversation and why didn't she answer when Zuri tried to contact her?

Zuri stood and paced the length of her

apartment, her wall of icons following her wherever she went, always keeping her in the center of her Personal Bubble.

Remembering one of their recent conversations, Zuri recalled the loss of their friend, Ann, to suicide. Zuri remembered how worn and tired Mae Lin had looked that day. And the way she'd talked about how hard it could be to live in Aspire.

Mae Lin would never commit suicide. Would she?

Zuri shook off that troubling thought. Everyone in Aspire lived on the edge. Most were artists of one type or another. Some were business entrepreneurs. No one had it easy, always struggling to keep their bills to a minimum and pay them on time.

The Monster Dash clock kept ticking down.

A robotic voice piped up to give the countdown. "This event begins in two minutes fifty-nine seconds, fifty-eight, fifty-seven..."

Zuri squeezed in one more attempt to contact Mae Lin, worried at her friend's continued failure to answer.

Mae Lin is fine. She's probably busy with something that came up.

But if something came up, why wouldn't Mae Lin let Zuri know about it? Mae Lin was one of the most responsible people Zuri had ever known. Mae Lin always kept Zuri posted about everything that happened, whether business or personal.

This doesn't make sense. It isn't like Mae Lin to be out of reach like this.

The robotic countdown continued. "One minute twenty-nine seconds, twenty-eight, twenty-seven..."

Zuri wanted to rush to the outskirts of VainGlory, hop into a drone taxi, and race back to Aspire. She'd check Mae Lin's apartment and then use a local device to scour her favorite places.

Remembering the day she'd first arrived in VainGlory, Zuri recalled how Donna had told her about the Privacy Wall surrounding the city. What if that wall had decided to block outsiders like Mae Lin? What if it now prevented Zuri's attempts to contact Mae Lin or her friend's responses?

"Five, four, three, two, one!"

The sound of a starting pistol startled Zuri out of her worries.

The marquee and the countdown clock burst into a puff of white smoke. The façade of a haunted house with shattered windows, weathered shutters, and overgrown in ivy dominated Zuri's field of vision, surrounded by the dark of night. The illusion of a full moon and bright stars reflected against the house and the stone path leading to its door.

Hundreds of bubbles filled with VainGlorians exploded into sight and rushed down the path and through the front door.

Zuri scanned the bubbles, hoping to see Mae Lin but sagged in disappointment.

The image displayed before Zuri switched to an overhead blueprint of the layout of the maze, which Benjamin had expanded to multiple levels in anticipation of a large crowd. The blueprint reduced in size and then separated into many blueprints, each showing a different level and the activity on it.

Still concerned, Zuri watched with half-hearted enthusiasm.

"Don't worry," Benjamin said, materializing at her side. "We'll find her."

For the first time, Zuri noticed the Soundtrack Benjamin had fashioned for the maze, now jam-packed with creaks and groans, sighs and screams, all underscored by disturbing organ music. "Well done, Ben," she said absent-mindedly.

"I think you have a success on your hands. Try to enjoy it."

Sharpening her attention, Zuri felt overwhelmed by what she saw. Vain-Glorians screamed their way through the maze, chased by monsters of all shapes and sizes that emerged from every crevice and around every corner. Magnificent mayhem dominated every level.

The image of an elegant gold-leaf picture frame floated at the perimeter of Zuri's vision, showing the image of Milan screaming while escaping the taloned fingers of a vampire.

"I think that means she's enjoying herself," Benjamin said.

In rapid succession, dozens of framed images of other VainGlorians filled the space around the blueprints. Dozens turned into hundreds, and they organized into tightly-packed groups.

"And I believe those are clusters," Benjamin continued.

Clusters.

Donna had told Zuri that earning her place in the Platinum Tower required achieving clusters, endorsements, and breaking trends.

If those are clusters, all I need is an endorsement and a breaking trend.

Zuri brightened with hope.

If I can get an endorsement and a breaking trend, then I can move into the Platinum Tower. And when that happens, I can bring Mae Lin to VainGlory. She'll be safe with me.

She turned to Benjamin. "What do I do? How can I get an endorsement? How do I make a breaking trend happen?"

"You don't. It has to happen organically."

Zuri wrung her hands. "That can't be right." She gestured toward the happy havoc infesting the blueprints. "There has to be something I can do."

"If people had influence on how customers respond, everyone would live in the Platinum Tower. What you want has to be earned. You can't buy it. You can't force it."

Feeling the sweat on her palms, Zuri wiped them against her clothes. "You mean all I can do is wait and see what happens?"

"That's right."

Zuri moaned as if someone had punched her in the stomach. "I can't bear it. I can't watch. There's too much at stake."

But before she could close her eyes or put a veil over the display, one of the elaborate frames broke free of its cluster and levitated below the blueprints. The frame showed a man with breath-taking magnetism grinning as he wrapped a vest fashioned by Mae Lin around his muscular forearm, wearing it like a sleeve. His grin widened when his arm acted like a machine gun, pelting silver bullets at a ferocious werewolf that howled and collapsed at his feet. Pumping his arm in the air, the man let out a whoop of delight.

"I recognize him," Zuri said in awe. "That's Shepard Green."

"A friend of yours?"

"No! He's the most famous quarterback in the country." Zuri paused, imagining that Personal Digital Assistants probably knew nothing of sports. "All famous athletes live in VainGlory, and Shepard Green is the most famous of all."

Her heart pounded with joy.

He's wearing something from our line. Shepard Green is wearing something Mae Lin designed.

Shepard Green flicked his wrist, and a large stamp appeared in his hand. He pumped it forward, and the word "Endorsed" stamped in bright red in front of his face.

"There's your first endorsement," Benjamin said.

Zuri shrieked with happiness, unable to speak.

Her display flipped back to show the façade of the haunted house, where hundreds more bubbles filled with VainGlorians popped into view and then stormed through the front door.

If Benjamin had been a real person, she would have grabbed his arm and clung to it in order to steady herself.

Still watching the façade of the haunted house, Zuri stared in wonder as countless VainGlorian bubbles streamed into view for what felt like a welcome eternity. While they continued to pour into the house, bright white sparks of light framed her field of vision. Those lights formed a banner that read "Breaking Trend."

Zuri stared in silent wonder. She wanted to scream in delight but couldn't find her voice.

"Hey," Shepard Green's voice called out. His bubble now floated on the stone path leading to the haunted house. "Can we connect?"

Without thinking, Zuri said, "Sure."

The bubble transformed into a life-size doorway. A room occupied with black furniture and walls made of screens filled with football game footage stood behind the famous man. He jerked a thumb outside the frame, back toward the haunted house. "You made that?"

Zuri felt as if her mouth took on a life of its own and spoke without her control. "Yes. Well, Ben did most of it, but I made the decisions."

Shepard Green frowned. "Ben? Who's that? Your boyfriend?"

"No!" Zuri shouted. She focused on bringing the volume of her voice to an acceptable level. Noticing how Shepard Green winced at her shout, she said, "Sorry. Sometimes the volume in my bubble goes out of control. Ben needs to fix it. He's not my boyfriend. He's my Personal Digital Assistant." She glanced at Benjamin, hoping she hadn't hurt his feelings and then realized that programs don't have feelings. Still, she felt bad about blaming her own stupid shouting on him.

"Great event," Shepard said. "Best I've been to in forever." He winked. "I endorsed it."

"I know!" Zuri shouted again. This time, she said, "Sorry. That was me, not my bubble. It's my first endorsement, and it means the world to me. You'll never know how much."

Shepard extended his hand. "Why don't you come over and tell me?"

Anxiety struck Zuri like an anvil dropped on her head.

She'd moved to Aspire at the age of 14 and had spent her life until now focused on work and striving to achieve success. She'd had only one boyfriend, and their relationship had never gone beyond the online stage.

Zuri now stared at Shepard Green, one of the most famous men in the country—on the planet. Everyone knew about his relationships, which sometimes changed weekly.

I don't compare to any of the women he's been with—they're all so beautiful and famous. I'm just me.

Maybe Shepard Green did this every time he gave an endorsement. Maybe he was like Milan, who had told Zuri how VainGlorians loved to discover new talent and how it brought them attention and credibility.

Surely, that's what this famous man wanted: more attention and more credibility.

Before Benjamin could weigh in, Zuri walked toward Shepard Green's doorway, took his hand, and walked into his world.

CHAPTER 21

The next morning, Zuri woke up with a start, not recognizing her surroundings. Panic seized her like a lost child.

Frozen with fear, Zuri took in the environment while she let herself come fully awake.

Under the soft cotton covers of an enormous canopy bed with square mahogany posts, a muscular naked man snored next to her.

Shepard Green. The football star. He invited me to his home after he endorsed my maze.

Gradual memories returned of how they ended up in his bed.

Light-hearted and happy music played on her Personal Soundtrack, but when Zuri tried to turn the volume down, nothing happened. With a start, Zuri realized her Personal Bubble appeared to be blocked. She saw none of the icons from her wall and no sign of Benjamin.

Then she remembered what Shepard Green had told her when she entered his bubble last night.

You can only be in one bubble at a time. If I come into your bubble, mine gets blocked. When you came into my bubble, yours was blocked. It's automatic. Personal Bubbles only show one reality at a time.

Zuri shivered, partly from delight and partly from anguish.

Did I do the right thing? Will anything come back to haunt me? What does he think of me? And how do I get out?

"Good morning." Yawning, Shepard Green rolled onto his side and faced her with a smile. "Sleep well?"

Flustered, Zuri managed to utter "Yes."

Shepard Green climbed out of bed, still naked, and strolled toward a bank of French doors lining the opposite wall. He opened a pair of doors to look outside, breathing in the fresh air. "I'm surprised you're still here. Do you need help getting home?"

His question startled the nervousness out of Zuri. She sat up in his bed, hugging the covers close against her chest. "Wait. When I came here last night, it was virtual. I don't remember leaving home. Am I still there?"

Shepard Green turned to face her again. "Of course."

More memories rushed back, but they confounded Zuri even more. "But ... last night. If I'm not here, how is last night possible?"

Shepard Green laughed and began to get dressed. He put on a shirt but left it open, still mostly naked. "Everything you see is real."

So confused that she forgot to be embarrassed, Zuri said, "I know. But I felt things. Everything I remember seems real. How can that be?"

Shepard Green didn't appear to be interested in wearing anything other than an open shirt. He walked around the bed as if strutting on a catwalk, which he sometimes did in his off-season modeling career. "No one told you about your Cuddle Bed? If they didn't tell you when you first arrived in the city, your PDA should have told you."

PDA. Personal Digital Assistant.

Benjamin.

Zuri shook her head in confusion.

Shepard Green grinned and gestured at his own bed. "It's great for sleeping. But when someone gets in it with me, it triggers a different mode." He shrugged. "I hear it's linked to your Personal Bubble, and there are a lot of things to trigger your brain into accepting what you see and feel as reality.

Tapping into memories and your fantasies and the like. I guess that's why it feels so real."

Discomfort washed through Zuri. Never having been in a situation like this before, she didn't know whether to feel elation or shame. A sudden urge to go back to something familiar took over. "You said you can help me go home. Can you do that right now?"

"Sure. Follow me." Shepard Green paraded past the bed toward the open doorway to a hallway.

Zuri looked around the room for the clothing she had worn last night but found none. Finding a light comforter folded at the foot of the bed, she wrapped it around herself before following the mostly-naked man leading the way.

At the end of a long hallway, he gestured toward the doorframe leading to the next room. That doorway gleamed bright white. Turning back to face Zuri, his eyebrows lifted in surprise to see her wrapped in his comforter. Smirking, he said, "It's pointless to take a souvenir. You'll be empty-handed when you get home."

"It's not that." Zuri felt uncomfortable where she stood and shifted her weight from one foot to the other and then back again. "I'm not used to this kind of thing."

"What kind—" Shepard Green halted before he could finish his question, and his expression softened in understanding. "Oh. I see."

When she took a step forward, he held out one hand, signaling her to stop.

"I was thinking," Shepard Green said. "Maybe we could get together again tonight."

Zuri sagged in disappointment before she could think to hide her feelings. Like everyone else on the planet, she'd heard a lot about Shepard Green's reputation with women.

Is that all I mean to him? Is that all he wants? From me or any other woman that catches his attention for the moment?

Because Zuri had spent so much of her life focused on achieving success, she had little interest in spending time with men likely to waste it. Such men would probably interfere with her goals. She'd seen many women in Aspire cave in to lust and get so sidetracked that they failed.

Zuri promised herself long ago that she'd never let anything so pointless and stupid happen to her.

And she'd promised Mae Lin that no man would ever come between their friendship and their dreams of success.

His face mirrored her concern. "We could talk. Or go somewhere. We can go anywhere from here without having to leave." He waved his hand at the doorway. The doorframe glowed yellow, and beyond it stood the Eiffel Tower surrounded by the streets of Paris. "We can go anywhere you want."

The change in Shepard Green's demeanor caught Zuri off guard, and more memories from last night rushed forward. She remembered laughing with him and enjoying his company. She remembered feeling at ease with him in a way she'd never experienced with a man before.

Had his behavior this morning been callous? Or had he simply felt a familiarity with her that she hadn't remembered or expected?

Zuri didn't know what to think. "I'll think about it," she said. "But I don't want to go to Paris now. I'd like to go home, if you don't mind helping me."

Shepard Green gave another wave to the doorframe. The Eiffel Tower beyond it disappeared, replaced by the familiar sight of Zuri's bedroom. "All you have to do is walk through."

Clutching the comforter tightly around her body, Zuri walked past him. As she walked through the doorway, she heard him call out, "Connect with me tonight?"

A shudder shook Zuri, and she found herself tangled in her own bedsheets, lying in her own bed.

She saw no trace of Shepard Green's comforter anywhere.

CHAPTER 22

As soon as Zuri got dressed and entered her living room, she dashed to the food delivery door and opened it, relieved to find her breakfast bag. Sinking onto her sofa to eat, Zuri couldn't help but notice the food was barely warm, a sure sign that she must be behind schedule.

The Incoming Connect icon pushed forward from the wall surrounding her. Before Zuri could answer, the image of a large cocoon swung in her living room, as if attached to the branch of a tree. Donna spoke, her voice sounding muffled as it came from inside the cocoon. "Congratulations on your first endorsement." Her tone took just a hint of a sneer. "And congratulations on snagging one of the most famous men in the world. You're officially a rising star."

Zuri blanched. How could Donna know?

The cocoon shuddered and swung like a pendulum. It broke loose from the invisible branch and landed on the floor of Zuri's living room with a sickening thud, cracking the sides of the cocoon.

With a tearing sound, the cocoon burst open.

A dragon the color of rubies emerged like a fresh chick and spread its paper-like wings out to dry. Donna spoke from its mouth. "This is an auspicious beginning for you. Take my advice: take advantage of everything your business partner creates. You've worn that bubble dress too often. Wear something different every day, and make sure all of your new fans see it. Change your outfit often throughout the day, and make sure they take notice. Make sure they talk about you. And then talk about them talking about you. And now that you have an influential boyfriend—"

"I don't think he's my boyfriend," Zuri blurted. "I've only seen him once."

"Then make sure you see him every day. This kind of boyfriend can launch you into real fame—the kind of fame he has—faster than you can image."

The idea startled Zuri.

Is that what I want? To have a relationship for the sake of achieving success?

At the same time, the opportunity that

faced her felt thrilling.

Zuri knew that opportunities like this were rare and usually fleeting.

Opportunities like this could come along once in a lifetime.

How could she snub it and live with the memory of what could have been?

The red dragon gained its strength. Climbing to its feet, the creature shook its wings and flapped them slowly. "One more thing," Donna said. "I keep my word." With that, she roared, and fire flamed from the dragon's mouth, burning the cocoon from which it had emerged into cinders. The dragon then glided through the doorframe and out of sight. The Incoming Connect icon faded back into the wall.

A knock rattled loudly against Zuri's front door.

Dread raced through her blood.

Is it Shepard Green? Did Donna convince him to come here?

When Zuri went to check the peephole, she discovered her front door had none. And the nearest window stood too far away to let her see who knocked outside.

Zuri took a deep breath to calm herself.

Donna said I'm a rising star. It's in her best interest to send someone who can help me. Would it be so terrible to have Shepard Green as a boyfriend? What if he isn't as bad as everyone thinks he is when it comes to women? What if he could help me?

Steeling her nerves, Zuri opened the door.

On the other side, Mae Lin grinned. "It took you long enough. Doesn't anyone in VainGlory know how to answer a knock on the door?"

CHAPTER 23

Zuri stood awash in a tsunami of relief and happiness and gratitude at the sight of Mae Lin.

Had they been back home in Aspire, Zuri would have nodded and gestured for her friend to come inside. Zuri might have then given Mae Lin a quick pat on the back or a brief hug.

The past days of worry caught up with Zuri. She'd felt lonely in VainGlory without her friend. The day Mae Lin shared the news of their friend Ann's suicide had cast a shroud of apprehension over Zuri and made her feel guilty for the sadness she saw on Mae Lin's face. Even worse, failing to find Mae Lin during the past few days had nagged at Zuri. Her greatest fear had been that Mae Lin had taken the same path as Ann, and Zuri didn't know how she could survive in the world without Mae Lin—not just as a business partner, but as her dearest friend.

With all that bubbling up inside, Zuri pulled Mae Lin inside and held her in a bear hug. Zuri's voice choked as she said, "I've missed you so much."

Mae Lin returned her hug but then tensed. "You're about to break my ribs!"

Startled by her own strength, Zuri let go and backed away. She shut the front door behind them and then grabbed Mae Lin's hand and pulled her into the living room and onto the sofa to sit next to Zuri. "Where have you been? I've been trying to reach you for days!"

Mae Lin gave her a blank look. "Here. I've been here in VainGlory."

Zuri returned her friend's blank look.

The wall of icons around Zuri became animated, and their chatter made it hard to hear Mae Lin. Zuri's Personal Soundtrack played a bright and lively song about success. Annoyed by it all, Zuri diminished the appearance of the icons and muted its sound as well as the soundtrack so she could hear her friend better.

"Didn't they tell you?" Mae Lin said.

"No." Zuri gathered her wits. "Why didn't you answer any of my connects?"

"I just arrived a few days ago. I've been in isolation ever since."

"Isolation?"

"It's protocol." Mae Lin frowned. "They put you in isolation when you first got here, didn't they?"

"No." Zuri thought back to her arrival. "When I got here, my new supervisor—our supervisor—met me. Donna took me to the Welcome Center. That's where I exchanged my Slim Goggles for a Personal Bubble and a Personal Digital Assistant."

"Oh!" Mae Lin said in exhilaration. "Isn't the PDA the best? Mine is named Worthington."

Her friend's enthusiasm surprised Zuri. "Since when do you get excited about things like that?"

Mae Lin smiled in chagrin. "I know. It's a little superficial of me, but it was awfully nice to feel like I had a friend by my side. They had a problem getting my Personal Bubble linked into the network. Thank goodness Worthington managed to work around it."

"That doesn't make sense." Zuri leaned back into the sofa, considering her friend's words. "It seems to me that a PDA has to have access to the network."

"Like I said, Worthington worked around it. I had no access to anything, but Worthington did."

"Your Personal Bubble was disconnected from the network but your PDA wasn't?"

"I suppose so."

Different trains of thoughts entered

Zuri's head as if it were a wheelhouse terminal.

After ten years of friendship and sharing a business, Zuri considered Mae Lin to be the most honest person she had ever known. Mae Lin believed lying to be pointless, because business couldn't run smoothly unless everyone involved knew the truth—and she extended that belief to all aspects of life.

Zuri saw no reason for Mae Lin to have been put in isolation during the past few days.

Unless there was a reason why someone in VainGlory didn't want Zuri to be in contact with Mae Lin.

But that made no sense either. Zuri had been busy creating the maze that would attract VainGlorians to Mae Lin's designs. She'd met Milan, who had helped Zuri with ideas. She'd met Shepard Green, who had given the first endorsement that had catapulted the maze into the spotlight, resounding as a huge success.

"Oh," Mae Lin said. "Donna came by my isolation pod early this morning to bring me over here. Before we left, she showed me how well you did last night." Mae Lin beamed. "Good job, Zuri!"

"Thanks." Zuri continued to struggle to find a reason why Mae Lin would be put in isolation and came up with nothing.

Mae Lin's eyes widened in wonder. "Is it

true Shepard Green is your boyfriend?"

"No!" Zuri said in protest. Reconsidering, she said, "I don't know."

"But you spent the night with him. I know you don't want to do that with anyone you're not serious about."

Fiercely private about such things, Mae Lin's knowledge of it chilled Zuri. "How do you know I spent the night with him?"

Unfazed, Mae Lin said, "When Donna showed me the success of last night's maze, all the icons around it were buzzing about you and Shepard. It's all over the network."

Zuri shuddered, wishing she'd never accepted his invitation.

Mae Lin leaned forward and squeezed Zuri's hand. "You worry too much!"

"Maybe. I don't want to make the same mistake I made with Roland."

Mae Lin laughed. "You won't. I have faith in you. This is nothing like the relationship you had with that engineer." She rolled her eyes. "What a loser he turned out to be—and that happened years ago. Shepard Green is different. Even if he's not right for you, it can't hurt to be with him for a while."

"I don't know. I'm not a free spirit like you. I don't know how to breeze in and out of relationships, and it's so easy for you."

Mae Lin raised a reproachful eyebrow. "What do you mean?"

Zuri scrambled to amend her statement. "Nothing bad. You understand relationships, whether it's business or friendship or romantic. It's harder for me. That's all."

Mae Lin's voice softened. "You'll be fine with Shepard Green. Just trust your gut. If something feels right, go with it. If it doesn't, get out as fast as you can."

"Donna wants me to spend a lot of time with him. To be seen. I don't know if it's the right thing to do."

Mae Lin shrugged. "Try it. What have you got to lose?" Once again animated, Mae Lin said, "Donna told me you should be wearing different outfits every day. Wait until you see the new designs I came up with when I was in isolation!"

Zuri watched while Mae Lin pulled her Design Pad from her pocketbook and opened a series of images to show her newest designs.

At the same time, Zuri tried to push away the nagging question of why Mae Lin had been put in isolation—and why no one had told Zuri about it.

* * *

Donna had become lost in the most recent set of statistics when an Incoming Connect dominated her field of vision. The ticker running at the bottom of the doorframe that announced the caller made her forget about the statistics. She pushed them aside and answered. "Mr. Buckingham. How can I help?"

The image of the man that materialized appeared paler and leaner than the last time she'd spoken to him. The past few months had aged him beyond his years.

"Be on the alert," Franklin Buckingham said.

"Is it time?"

"Not quite. But it will be soon." He paused. "Is everything in place?"

"Yes, even better than expected. The bonus has come through."

"Bonus? What bonus?"

Donna smiled. "The business partner. I brought her to VainGlory after noticing how pretty she is. The girl is even prettier in person."

Franklin Buckingham perked up. "Show me."

Donna brought up an image.

Franklin Buckingham dismissed it. "Not for me."

"Maybe not," Donna said, "but she'll catch someone's eye."

CHAPTER 24

For the next few weeks, Zuri reveled in her new-found success.

At the suggestion made by a jewelry store that caught her attention inside her Personal Bubble, Zuri treated herself by buying a diamond bracelet. Wearing it night and day, her growing ambition sparkled like every diamond captured around her wrist.

Success felt good.

Each day when she climbed out of bed and opened her wall of icons, Zuri found her business site swarmed with customers. Their bubbles jammed around the site, while they walked their own catwalks and modeled which of Mae Lin's outfits they'd bought.

Everyone talked so loud and so fast that Zuri rarely understood anything they said, so she made a habit of nodding and smiling in response.

Success felt too good to worry about minor details like not understanding every little thing anyone said.

In the afternoons, Zuri went site-hopping with her new best friend Milan, who insisted on introducing Zuri to the most influential residents of VainGlory.

Taking Donna's advice to heart, Zuri changed her outfit a few times every day, always sporting one of Mae Lin's new designs and showing them off to Milan's fancy friends and acquaintances. As a result, endorsements increased. Clusters grew. And nearly every outfit Zuri wore became a breaking trend, and she moved higher and higher inside the Platinum Tower, now just a few floors from the penthouse.

Success felt so good that Zuri wanted to drown in it.

Every evening, Shepard Green escorted Zuri to a different hot spot: Paris, Rome, London, Barcelona, Prague. Wherever they arrived, all eyes trended toward them.

They danced in clubs through the night, allowing fans to surround them with attention. Like her wall of icons, the fans shouted over each other, but the blasting music made it impossible for Zuri to hear any of them.

Like always, she smiled and nodded at

them, often throwing in a friendly wave for good measure. Each time, Zuri admired the brilliance with which her diamond bracelet sparkled when she waved.

Every few days, Zuri connected with Mae Lin, who became so fascinated by her Personal Digital Assistant's guidance that she struggled to stay focused on any conversation. One day, Zuri became so concerned that she said, "What's going on?"

Trendy music emanated from Mae Lin's image inside the Outgoing Connect doorframe. Zuri assumed it was her friend's latest Personal Soundtrack, but it seemed to consume her attention. Mae Lin giggled and became sidetracked talking to her Personal Digital Assistant, Worthington, which took the shape of a robotic seahorse that hovered in mid-air.

"Mae Lin!" Zuri shouted to get her attention. "Is there a problem?"

The seahorse spun to look at Zuri.

Mae Lin's happy expression deflated. "Why are you so shouty?"

"Because I've been asking questions that you're not answering."

The seahorse spun back to face Mae Lin, who laughed at something it said so softly that Zuri couldn't hear. Turning her attention to Zuri, Mae Lin said, "You should come over. We're having an opium tea party."

Opium.

Despite the uptick in Zuri's social life, she'd kept a promise she and Mae Lin had made to each other ten years ago. No matter what, they decided to keep their distance from any substance that could affect their business.

"Opium," Zuri said. "That's not what we decided. That's not what we promised."

Mae Lin's face fell blank for a moment, and then she scrunched her nose in annoyance. "Oh, Zuri, don't be so boring."

"When I make a promise, I keep it."

Mae Lin groaned in mock agony. "That was eons ago. Things are different now. Haven't you noticed?"

The diamond bracelet felt cold against Zuri's skin.

Zuri's concern for her friend deepened by the moment. "We still have a business to run."

"The business is fine! We've made enough money to last a lifetime. Relax, Zuri. All the hard work is over. Now all we have to do is enjoy what we've accomplished." Mae Lin waved with a grin. "Lighten up. Remember, fame is the name of the game. And we've already won. We don't have to play the game anymore."

Mae Lin then blinked out of sight, and the Outgoing Connect icon faded back and nestled among the hundreds of other icons crowding Zuri's wall.

Zuri considered everything Mae Lin

said.

Even if they never made another sale, Mae Lin had spoken the truth when she said they now had enough money to last for the rest of their lives. It was also true that they'd risen into the highest echelons of fame.

Maybe she's right. Maybe it is time to enjoy what we've achieved.

Although Zuri continued following Donna's advice to change outfits throughout the day and comment on her customers' comments, Zuri began to take it easy. She felt as if she were swimming in money and glory, drinking all of it in.

Without realizing it, she began to feel superior to all the artists she'd left behind in the city of Aspire. She smirked at the memory of Karen and how that woman had tried to undermine Zuri. Good riddance to Karen and her pitiful home of Ascend, to which she'd returned with her tail tucked between her legs.

Zuri considered herself too smart to make the mistakes Karen had made.

Spending more and more time with Milan, Zuri connected with Mae Lin less often.

One day, Zuri's attempt to connect resulted in seeing a Do Not Disturb notice that popped up inside the Outgoing Connect icon.

Upset by it, Zuri poured out her heart

to Milan. "She's my best friend! We're like sisters."

Sharing a drink at the bar located at the highest point in VainGlory, a circular room surrounded by windows, Milan crossed her arms. "I thought I was your best friend."

Zuri attempted to recover her good graces with the VainGlorian. "Of course, you are. What I mean to say is that Mae Lin is my oldest friend. She was my best friend when we lived in Aspire."

"But you don't live in Aspire anymore. And you're not a struggling artist anymore." Milan sipped from a tall glass filled with turquoise alcohol. "Don't take it personally. Things change for people like you who come to VainGlory."

People like you.

People who aren't native VainGlorians. People who have to struggle to earn wealth because they aren't born with it.

"Oh," Zuri said, unable to hide the hurt in her voice. Silently, she wondered who Mae Lin could have met and be willing to get close to so quickly.

CHAPTER 25

"Come on," Shepard Green said as they stood on top of the Great Pyramid on the Giza Plateau, a short distance from Cairo. "It'll be fun."

Standing on the rough stone apex, Zuri felt queasy at the sight of the distant desert sand below, where a small group of men wearing long white gowns waved frantically, possibly as a warning. "I don't know."

Zuri had grown fond of Shepard, happy for his constant companionship and lavish attention. She worried that he talked little about himself, which made her wonder how well she knew him. Despite that one concern, for the first time in her life, Zuri wondered if she had fallen in love.

But falling in love didn't mean she had to fall off a 47-story-high stone structure to prove her feelings for anyone.

Zuri's nervous fingers adjusted her diamond bracelet. The sparkling stones caught the powerful Egyptian sunlight and cast it toward her eyes, blinding Zuri for a moment.

"I dare you," Shepard said. Grinning, he spread the paper wings attached to the harness strapped around his chest. Looking like aged parchment, they crackled against the wooden framework that held them together, like the bones of a pterodactyl. "Last one down is a rotten egg." Giving a wild yelp, he jumped into empty air.

Zuri let loose a cry of terror without realizing she'd done it. She clung to the nearest stone to keep her balance while watching Shepard.

The athlete glided away from the pyramid with ease, sailing alongside the three pyramids that formed a line on the plateau.

The group of gowned men raced beneath him, still shouting as Shepard whooped and hollered with glee.

A whirling column of dust caught Zuri's attention as it traveled from behind her and toward Shepard's path.

In a moment of dread, she wondered if the gowned men on the desert floor had seen it approaching. Had those men shouted and waved with the intent of warning Zuri and Shepard?

Zuri crouched and held on tight to the stone as wind buffeted all around her. For a few moments, it threatened to rip her into its dangerous embrace.

Those moments passed. Zuri turned her attention to the continuing path of the whirling dust. Her throat tightened with dread when she saw it aim for Shepard.

"Shepard!" Zuri cried out.

The whirling dust caught Shepard before he could glide down toward the desert. The column spun him head over heels, ripping his paper wings into shreds and the wooden frame into splinters.

The dust spit Shepard out, and he plummeted to the hard sand floor below.

Zuri screamed and stared in disbelief at Shepard's motionless body, looking like a broken marionette.

How do I get down? How do I get to Shepard?

But then the truth dawned on Zuri.

This isn't real. We're not in Egypt. We're inside Shepard's home, like always. He's fine. Nothing's wrong. All I have to do is figure out how to get back.

She turned in place, looking all around her until she saw the glimmering doorway and Shepard's hallway leading to his bedroom beyond it.

But the doorway stood several feet from the edge of this level of the pyramid. They had first climbed onto it several feet below.

Zuri looked at the downward climb she now faced. She'd only been able to ascend the enormous stone blocks with Shepard's help. Descending on her own would involve a series of steep drops.

"Shepard!" she called out to the doorway leading back to his home. "Where are you?"

His failure to answer worried Zuri.

She imagined he might be fetching lunch from his delivery door. Or he might be in the bathroom. Or he might have received an important Incoming Connect from his coach or agent.

Still, concern gnawed at the back of Zuri's thoughts.

Not willing to take the time to descend the pyramid, Zuri edged her way to the other side of the pyramid's apex and took the few steps possible to give her a running leap. One foot grazed the edge of the doorframe, accidentally kicking her away from a safe landing.

Falling, she made a desperate grab with her hands, catching the doorframe before she could plunge beneath it.

Heart racing, Zuri drew upon all the willpower and faith in herself she'd developed in Aspire. With a guttural yell to gather strength and fortitude, she hauled herself up and onto the safety of the floor of Shepard's bedroom.

But when Zuri looked up, she saw no sign of Shepard Green.

*　*　*

Zuri sprinted down the hallway into her boyfriend's bedroom. "Shepard! Where are you?"

The bedroom stood empty.

She found the adjacent bathroom empty, as well.

Zuri ran into the hallway, ready to check the rest of Shepard's home.

But the doorway at the end of the hallway still displayed the side of the pyramid in Egypt. Zuri stopped at its edge and yelled through the doorway. "Shepard!"

The only response she heard was the sound of men yelling in Arabic.

A light, warm breeze tickled her skin. Its touch caught Zuri's attention, because it didn't come from the other side of the doorway, where the desert weather was hot and dry.

The breeze came from behind her. From the bedroom.

Zuri crept back into that room, following the feel of the breeze, now drifting into her face. Setting foot back inside the bedroom, she said, "Shepard?"

Two of the French doors opposite the bed stood open, letting the breeze inside.

Zuri approached the open doors, never having given that much attention to them before. Stepping close, she saw they opened up onto a balcony.

Nausea tickled the back of Zuri's throat. "No," she said. "It's impossible." She stood still for several minutes, not wanting to take another step.

The incoming breeze buffeted her face, and Zuri felt as if she were waking up from a bad dream. With conviction, she said, "It's not possible. I'll prove it."

Zuri stepped outside on the balcony and looked down, only to see Shepard Green's body sprawled on the pavement 200 stories below, broken and lying in a river of his own blood.

Zuri screamed, clinging to the balcony railing for life.

CHAPTER 26

Zuri ran back into her boyfriend's bedroom and shouted for his wall of icons, currently dimmed in the background, to come forward. "Outgoing Connect!" she yelled. "Call for help now!"

His wall failed to respond.

"This is an emergency! Listen to me. Call for help right now. Shepard needs help!"

Still, no response.

"Stupid!" Zuri screamed at the wall. "Emergencies override everything. What's wrong with you?" Giving up on his wall, Zuri ran back down the hallway, desperate to get home and back inside her own Personal Bubble where she could send for help.

She pulled up short at the sight of the pyramid, still on the other side of the doorframe at the end of the hallway. Going back to Egypt would do no good. She'd be stuck on top of a pyramid, and she didn't know how to call for help from there.

"Go away!" Zuri shouted at the pyramid. "I need to get help!"

The image shimmered into blackness.

Zuri hesitated, not knowing what to do. Whenever she'd used this doorway as a portal back to her home and Personal Bubble, it had displayed the sight of her own bedroom. If it were night, she'd understand. But during the middle of the day, she should be able to see her room clearly.

A bubble filled with light floated in the darkness. Milan's face appeared inside the bubble.

"Milan!" Zuri shouted in relief. "Thank God! I need help! Call for help!"

Her VainGlorian friend spoke in a soothing voice. "I know, Honey. It's already been done."

As if on cue, a siren sounded in the distance.

Zuri sank to her knees in relief and cried for the first time.

"Your scream shook all of VainGlory to its core. I think the whole city heard it."

Through her sobs, Zuri said, "I don't know what happened. I don't know how it *could* have happened. We passed through to Egypt, but that was in his living room. How could he have still been with me if he went back to his bedroom? He would have had to go back through the passageway, the doorframe between his living room and the hallway."

Milan shushed her. "Don't worry about that now. There's plenty of time to think about it once you've had time to collect yourself." Milan extended one hand through the edge of the bubble containing her image. "You shouldn't be alone right now. Let me help."

Zuri brushed her tears away, even though she still cried. She stood, grateful at the thought of being with someone who cared.

Before Zuri could take Milan's hand, the breeze from Shepard's bedroom skimmed over her shoulders, making Zuri shudder.

A new thought occurred to her.

Why can't I see Milan's home? That what I always see when I go into her Personal Bubble. Why is everything around her so dark? And why is she floating inside a bubble? That's how my customers are shown when they visit my business site.

Zuri felt her skin crawl.

Milan's image flickered briefly. Her tone turned condescending. "You're in shock, Honey. Let me take care of you."

Zuri thought about her friend Ann, who committed suicide in Aspire.

Zuri considered how Mae Lin had

changed since arriving in VainGlory. Zuri had assumed they'd spend most of their time together, but every day Mae Lin vanished more and more from Zuri's life.

Zuri remembered what Karen said the day after being attacked by a shark and deciding to return to her home in Ascend.

I know they say fame is the name of the game, but it's not worth dying for. Is it?

Without knowing why, Zuri bolted away from the doorframe leading to Milan's Personal Bubble and back into Shepard's bedroom, slamming the door shut behind her.

What can I do? I'm 200 stories high. There's no way beyond this room. How do I get out of here?

Trembling, Zuri sank onto the edge of the bed, trying to calm her nerves when reality slapped her in face.

I'm not really here. This is Shepard's Personal Bubble, and I'm sharing it. All I have to do is figure out a way to see it.

Benjamin.

Her Personal Digital Assistant couldn't communicate with her when she was inside someone else's Personal Bubble.

But Zuri's body was in her apartment in the Platinum Tower, not in Shepard's luxurious home. Surely, Benjamin had heard her every time she'd spoken out loud. Maybe he was the one who had sent an ambulance or the police—not Milan.

Thinking about everything she'd said

out loud, Zuri realized she'd spoken only about needing help, not about her predicament. Benjamin had no way of knowing she couldn't find her way out of Shepard's bubble.

No longer crying, Zuri decided to talk to Benjamin out loud, hoping he would hear her. "Ben, I need you. I'm trapped inside Shepard's Personal Bubble, and there's no way out. Most of the time, I use his bedroom doorway to get home, but we went to Egypt on the spur of the moment. Everything is stuck the way he set it up. Right now, his bedroom doorway opens up to the hallway, and the end of the hallway opens up to Egypt. Except, that portal went black, and Milan floated inside a bubble. She told me to come to her, but it felt wrong."

Zuri shivered again and continued. "I'm scared, Ben. Can you get me out of here? Can you put a portal in his bedroom doorway that will bring me back home?"

She wished she could hear Benjamin's voice and take comfort in his pale green eyes, but Shepard's Personal Bubble made that impossible.

All she could do was hope.

Zuri knew it would take little more than a split-second for Benjamin to set up a portal if he had heard her, but she hesitated to open Shepard's bedroom door. She dreaded the thought that the black gateway at the end of the hallway had moved forward and that she'd be facing Milan's strange image again.

Swallowing the fear that tightened her throat, Zuri turned the doorknob of the bedroom door and eased it open a crack.

At the sight of her own home, Zuri threw the door open and ran across the threshold.

Zuri's own Personal Bubble rushed into place, surrounding her with the wall of icons. It throbbed with hundreds of weeping fans, all holding up signs reading "We're with you, Zuri," "You tried to save him," and "We love you."

Zuri's Personal Soundtrack swelled with an orchestra playing a melancholy song.

When Zuri saw her Personal Digital Assistant materialize in his robot form, she rushed into his arms, leaning into his image even though she couldn't feel him. "I love you, Ben," Zuri whispered, not caring that his existence boiled down to something binary instead of flesh and blood. "I love you so much."

Benjamin whispered, "I love you, too, Zuri."

A loud knock on the front door jolted Zuri. "Who is it?" she called out.

"VainGlory Police."

Flush with relief at the thought of doing something to help, Zuri hurried to the door and opened it.

Two men wearing dark suits and grim expressions stared at her. "Zuri Blacksheep?"

"Yes," she said. "I'm so glad you're here. Please come in."

The man who had spoken cleared his throat. "We'd like you to come downtown with us."

The icons on Zuri's wall shouted protests on her behalf and then hurled insults at the men in suits.

The other man pointed at her wall of icons. "Please remove your Personal Bubble and hand it to me."

CHAPTER 27

Zuri wriggled in her chair in the interrogation room, finding it impossible to find a comfortable position. The room stood smaller than even a modest walk-in closet. A small round table separated her from the seated detectives, all of them crammed between the walls and the table. "I've already told you a dozen times," she said.

"Tell us again."

Once more, Zuri told them how Shepard had wanted to try gliding from the top of the Great Pyramid on a whim. Once more, she explained how she'd tried to dissuade him, only to see him get caught up in an unexpected dust storm that broke his gliding wings. Once more, she described how she escaped the virtual fantasy in Egypt, returned to her boyfriend's Personal Bubble to discover he'd fallen from the balcony of his home, and how she'd returned home to her own bubble.

"He committed suicide?" one detective said.

Unaccustomed to speaking to strangers, especially in such a strained environment, Zuri kept her arms crossed and her head down, too distressed to look in their eyes. "No. Shepard would never do that."

"Had he been depressed? Worried about his career?" The detective's voice took a dark tone. "He's getting old for a football player. Maybe he was afraid of losing his job."

Zuri snorted. "He wasn't afraid of anything. Thus, gliding off the top of a pyramid."

"You're getting a lot of attention because of it."

For a moment, Zuri forgot her aversion to being in such close proximity to strangers and having to talk to them. She looked up sharply to meet their eyes and said, "Excuse me?"

The other detective gave a casual shrug. "You're the gal who punched the shark, right?" He checked his notes. "That happened when you first arrived. At an event where you competed with other people that make clothes." He gave Zuri a look cool enough to make her shiver. "That was convenient."

"Convenient?" Zuri blurted. "That

shark almost killed Karen. And me! Besides, it wasn't a competition. It was just a show to introduce all of us."

The first detective nodded. "And you stole the show."

The accusation fueled a fire in Zuri's belly. "What should I have done? Let Karen die? Run away like everyone else?"

The second detective leaned forward and rested his arms on the tiny table separating them. "Of course not. That took a lot of courage. It's just hard not to notice how much you benefitted from it."

Agitated by the mounting blame in his eyes, Zuri sank into herself and stared down at her lap. "There's no way I could know what would happen after that show. I wasn't thinking about it when I ran to help Karen. I was too busy wondering how to save her life."

"Which is why we find it so surprising that you agreed to a stunt like gliding off the top of a pyramid."

"I didn't know that's what Shepard was going to do." Zuri shifted uncomfortably against her chair's hard surface. "I didn't find out until he actually did it." A new thought gave her hope, and she dared to look directly at the detectives again. "You took my Personal Bubble. There's got to be some kind of record of what happened. There must be security cameras all over VainGlory."

The first detective took a friendly tone. "Sure, but security cameras work in real life only. When you meet anyone inside their Personal Bubble, the only thing a security camera could record would be you inside your own home."

"Right," Zuri said, thinking it through. "But when I lived in Aspire, I used Slim Goggles. They record everything you see in them. It's automatic. Personal Bubbles are far more advanced. Why wouldn't they make recordings, too?"

The detectives exchanged questioning looks.

"Please," Zuri said. "There's got to be a way you can play back what I saw—what I experienced—with Shepard."

The first detective looked up at the corner of the room behind Zuri. "Can we do that?"

She followed his gaze and saw a small black camera mounted in that corner.

"Sure," a disembodied voice said. "Pop them in the reviewer."

The second detective jerked his arms off the table top when a small panel slid open to reveal a smooth surface with two divots. He then pulled the contact lenses he'd taken from Zuri and placed them on that surface. Moments later, a visual and audio recording of Zuri's point of view filled the walls, ceiling, and floor of the room.

For a moment, Zuri closed her eyes and

covered her ears with her hands, not wanting to re-live that awful event. She felt the rumble of voices through the soles of her shoes.

In that moment, Zuri realized she needed to see what the detectives saw, no matter how painful.

Gathering her courage, she opened her eyes and saw everything as she remembered it, starting with seeing the image of herself following Shepard Green through the door in his home to the pyramid and ending with the moment she found her way back home.

"Would you be willing to face a lie detector?"

"Yes," Zuri said without hesitation. "I have nothing to hide."

Her chair transformed as its arms opened and wrapped around her biceps.

Another panel on the table top slid open, and a robot that looked like a bee flew out of it and hovered in front of Zuri's face.

"Did you love him?" the first detective said.

Staring at the image of Benjamin, the final image still displayed from her Personal Bubble, Zuri assumed the detective refered to her Personal Digital Assistant. She remembered the relief she'd felt after coming home.

"Yes," Zuri said.

"Truth!" the robot bee announced.

The detectives proceeded to ask all the same questions she'd answered before, but this time the robot bee confirmed her claims, while the detectives studied her vital signs displayed in the air above the table.

For good measure, Zuri said, "Why don't you check the Personal Bubble of Shepard Green, too? It'll back up everything I'm telling you."

Ignoring her, the first detective said, "Interrogation concluded. You're free to go." He hesitated and then added, "For now."

After the detectives exited the room, Zuri began to leave in a huff, but not before she remembered to take the contacts for her Personal Bubble from the table.

It wasn't until she walked back inside her apartment in the Platinum Tower that Zuri placed the contacts in her eyes and brought up her Personal Bubble, stunned by what greeted her.

CHAPTER 28

As usual, hundreds of icons of Zuri's favorite people and places filled the wall surrounding her.

For the first time, their frames and backgrounds flashed black with disapproval. When the people inside those icons spotted Zuri, they shouted angrily at her. Although she couldn't make out the words, the hostile expressions on their faces cut her to the core.

"I don't understand," Zuri said to all of them. "What have I done to make you so mad?"

The volume skyrocketed as angry shouts turned to screams of rage.

Zuri cowered and backed away. But, like always, the wall followed her.

A news icon burst forward, where a newscaster glared at Zuri and shouted,

"You killed him! You're responsible for the death of Shepard Green!"

Shocked and horrified, Zuri said, "That's not true. I tried to save him."

The newscaster leaned across the desk and reached out as if meaning to strangle Zuri. "Liar!"

The hundreds of icons now flashed angry red backgrounds, still framed in black. At first shouting over each other, their voices joined in unison.

"Liar! Liar! Liar!"

Her Personal Soundtrack rumbled forward, consisting of dark music punctuated by cracks of lightning.

"But the police have cleared me," Zuri insisted as she fumbled to mute her soundtrack. "They've seen my Personal Bubble. They witnessed what happened. I even faced a lie detector."

The newscaster gestured to push a screen forward from the newsroom icon. The screen enlarged to stand between the wall of icons and Zuri. It then displayed Shepard's point of view, gazing down the side of the pyramid and across the Sahara Desert. His gaze stopped at Zuri, her faced strained with hatred.

"What?" Zuri said in surprise. "This isn't right."

Screaming, the image of Zuri stepped forward and shoved both hands at him.

"Zuri! No!" Shepard cried before he

tumbled down the pyramid, the image recording the fall from his eyes until landing on his back with a thud on the desert floor, facing the pyramid with Zuri still in sight at its apex.

The image then shifted, showing the side of the building where Shepard lived and a tiny image of Zuri looking down from his balcony.

"No!" Zuri said, trembling. "That's not what happened."

The large screen evaporated, and the newscaster crawled over the news desk as if coming after Zuri. "She lives in the Platinum Tower," the newscaster said. "Everyone who wants justice for Shepard Green, go and get her now!"

Neon-bright words flashed in mid-air: *Lynch her!*

With a shriek, Zuri pushed the wall of icons into the background, now barely visible. Standing in her living room, she looked for Benjamin but saw him nowhere. Not wanting any of the icons to hear her, Zuri whispered, "Ben, where are you?"

The robotic man materialized next to her, his pale green eyes pulsating. Like Zuri, he kept his voice low. "It's time to go. I can get you to safety. Meet me at the place where you first landed." Benjamin then blinked out of sight.

Her Personal Soundtrack grew in volume as if of its own accord, now playing the suspenseful type of music Zuri would expect to hear during a horror movie. She raised her voice slightly above the music. "Ben? Come back!"

"Right here, Miss." Benjamin now appeared in front of her, now displaying bright yellow eyes.

For a moment, Zuri thought of traffic lights changing from green to amber, from "go" to "caution."

Benjamin cocked his metallic head to one side. "Are you quite alright, Miss?"

The bright tone of his voice sickened Zuri, although she didn't know why.

A memory popped into her head. A memory of a locked box behind a locked door in her own virtual storage space.

While Benjamin had figured out how to open the door, neither of them had been able to unlock the box.

A box addressed to the wealthiest man in VainGlory. A box with a notation of Zuri's name on its label.

Zuri felt as if someone flipped a switch inside her.

I have to get out.

"I'd like some time alone," Zuri said in the most convincing voice she could muster. "Could you please diminish everything in my Personal Bubble and make sure no one disturbs me? I need to get some rest."

"I suppose," Benjamin said, his voice fraught with worry. "But do you think this is the best moment to rest?"

"Go away, Ben." Zuri snapped her fingers at him, and the robotic man disappeared. True to his word, her Personal Soundtrack dulled to a barely discernable murmur, and the wall of icons looked like a sheet of gauze, allowing most of the real environment behind it to bleed through.

Zuri wondered if she should take anything with her but decided that if people really were coming to lynch her that she needed every moment to escape. Still surrounded by the gauze-like wall, she ran out to her balcony and circled around the tower to step into the nearest elevator, perched on the exterior wall of the tower. Zuri peered through its glass walls and looked at the city below as the elevator descended. Relieved, she saw no one on the ground below.

What had Benjamin said before he reverted back to the way he was when she first met him?

Meet me at the place where you first landed.

The harbor in the water garden.

Once the elevator thudded to stop at ground level, Zuri stepped outside and stood at the foot of the tower, gazing around to gain her bearings.

The Platinum Tower dominated the heart of the city, encircled by rings of towers of gold, silver, and bronze. Zuri felt as if she stood in the center of a maze.

A few delivery drones buzzed among the towers, but the streets and sidewalks were mostly empty. A pair of women walked away from Zuri, followed by flat-bed robots bearing arms shaped like spades, rakes, and shears.

Zuri imagined the women were city gardeners.

Distant shouts startled Zuri, and she looked toward the sound, seeing no one.

They're coming after me. Everyone who used to love me is now trying to kill me.

Terrified, Zuri kept close to the edge of the Platinum Tower and followed its curve away from the oncoming voices, rabid with rage.

She caught a glimpse of the women gardeners as they rounded a corner and threaded their way between the rows of towers. They paused, and another flat-bed robot scuttled from a side street to catch up with them. But instead of being armed with gardening tools, this robot carried a pile of transparent objects that sparkled in a thin stream of sunlight.

The Carnival of Animals.

Zuri remembered the city park where the crystal animals roamed. It was where her launch had taken place, where Zuri had punched the shark that attacked Karen. Zuri didn't know how many parks existed in the city, but she knew of only one that had crystal animals.

And if she could find the Carnival of Animals, it would lead her to the water garden at the edge of the harbor where she'd first landed.

Not wanting to spook the women or place them in danger, Zuri raced down a sidewalk running parallel to their path. At every intersection, Zuri peeked around the corner until she saw the women emerge and continue along their way.

The angry shouts faded behind her.

Without warning, Zuri's wall of icons exploded back into full view. Angry faces fenced her in. The newscaster who had threatened Zuri pointed with fierce aggression at her and shouted, "There she is! She's escaped the tower!"

Zuri cowered in fear, frozen at the sight of hundreds of frightening faces looming around her.

Then she remembered she didn't have to look at them. Zuri pushed both hands at the wall, forcing it back to its former ghostly state. "Ben!" she shouted.

Her Personal Digital Assistant emerged and hurried to walk along her side as Zuri continued her parallel journey by the gardeners. "Miss? Are you quite alright?"

"No." She pointed at the gauze-like wall encircling her. "Don't ever let that happen again."

"Miss?" Benjamin's yellow eyes quivered. "I'm not sure I comprehend."

"People are coming to lynch me. You showed them where I am. Why would you do that?" Zuri increased her pace.

"Perhaps there's been some type of misunderstanding. No one means to harm you. I sense they might have some questions and would appreciate your answering them."

Zuri snorted in response. "Go away, Ben."

"Please, Miss. I'm certain we can discover a solution."

Zuri glared at the metallic man striding beside her. "Go away now. Don't bother me again, and don't let this wall change. Understand?"

Benjamin's voice sagged in disappointment. "Yes, Miss. Of course, Miss." He blinked out of sight.

However, the shouts in the far distance behind Zuri began getting louder.

Instead of pausing at the next corner, Zuri rushed ahead while considering the layout of the city.

If the Platinum Tower stood at its center, then streets and sidewalks radiated from it like spokes from a wheel. That meant with every block she ran forward, the distance between her sidewalk and the one traveled by the gardeners grew. And as the sidewalk Zuri now walked carried her farther from the gardeners, it would also increase the distance between Zuri and the

Carnival of Animals once the women arrived there.

At the next intersection, Zuri turned the corner and headed toward the sidewalk where she'd last seen the gardeners.

The faded wall of icons around her trembled as if caught in an earthquake.

Zuri paused and looked around, ready to admonish Benjamin the moment she saw him.

But her Personal Digital Assistant failed to appear.

When Zuri took another step, her wall shivered again. Walking slower now, Zuri studied everything around her. Gleaming towers with restaurants and stores wedged between them. Delivery drones speeding in and out of those establishments. Looking up, Zuri saw the sidewalk lined with streetlamps.

In unison, they turned their curved necks toward Zuri. But instead of light bulbs, the head of each streetlamp gleamed with the eye of a camera. A red light—the kind of light to indicate the beginning of a recording—glowed briefly above each camera eye.

They've found me. They know where I am.

Thrumming with adrenaline, Zuri ignored them and sped toward the next intersection. Looking one way, she saw the gardeners a block behind. Turning the opposite way, Zuri ran as fast as she could, ignoring the new row of streetlamps turning to face her. Now, between soaring buildings, she caught a glimpse of green up ahead.

The Carnival of Animals! I'm almost there.

Her rasping breath and pounding heart filled her ears. Zuri's aching legs begged her to stop. But she still heard the horrible cries far behind her.

Refusing to slow down, Zuri ran until she entered the Carnival of Animals, recognizing its lush lawns at once. Up ahead, she spotted the bridge where designers had modeled their creations and Karen had been attacked by a shark.

Walking with the thought of being safe here, the sight of more streetlamps scattered throughout the park startled Zuri.

Why didn't I notice them before? How did I not know so many of them were here?

Quickening her pace, dread filled Zuri when the streetlamps turned in her direction.

A crystal pig stepped onto the sidewalk in front of her and grunted. Its eyes glowed red for a moment.

Zuri's gauzy wall of icons shuddered.

They're cameras. The pig's eyes are cameras.

Not knowing where else to go, Zuri continued forward but the pig stood its ground.

It pawed at the sidewalk, chipping its crystal foot. Grunting deeper, it took a threatening stance.

Far behind the pig, a herd of crystal deer came into sight.

Zuri darted off the sidewalk to one side of the pig.

Following her direction, the pig ran to block her new path, only to catch its chipped foot on the edge of the sidewalk and tumble into the grass. When momentum rolled the pig onto its back, the crystal animal squealed in dismay.

Stopping short, Zuri ran to the opposite side and toward the bridge. Skidding to a stop, she ducked underneath the bridge, hiding from the streetlamps, the pig, and the herd of deer.

Her chest heaved, winded from racing. Her blood pounded against her temples, making Zuri feel like someone had put her head in a vise. Her legs ached, not wanting to move again.

What do I do now?

"Truly, Miss," Benjamin said, popping into view next to the bridge. "I do wish you would let me assist you."

Zuri thought she heard the whirr of streetlamps turning toward the sound of Benjamin's voice, even though he existed inside her Personal Bubble. Then she heard the clatter of hooves crossing the sidewalk, seeming to come in her direction. She held a silencing hand toward Benjamin and listened with intent.

The shouts of the mob pursuing her sounded louder.

While keeping her Personal Soundtrack and all other clamor from her icons muted, Zuri brought her wall out of suspension in order to track what was happening.

Banners filled the wall, reading:
Track her down!
String her up!
Kill Zuri!

The individual icons now meshed together, bringing everyone inside them into a united mob, which thrummed and made Zuri's entire wall vibrate. The crowd appeared to be running down the same sidewalk that Zuri had taken, currently located by the innermost towers surrounding the Platinum Tower.

They stopped running and stood together, everyone looking in a different direction. A young man gazed from the wall of icons until he locked eyes with Zuri. "There she is!" he shouted. "I found her!"

"Miss, please!" Benjamin said.

The herd of deer nosed around him, sniffing at empty air.

"Stop it!" Desperate, Zuri took the contacts out of her eyes, throwing them onto the ground beneath the bridge and stomping on them with her shoes.

Her Personal Bubble evaporated, and

the sense of utter aloneness stunned Zuri into silence.

No longer seeing Benjamin or the wall of icons, Zuri reached up and steadied her hands against the underside of the bridge above.

The herd of deer started at Benjamin's sudden disappearance, staring into space as if something magical had happened.

Are they going to hurt me?

Zuri stood still, wondering how to defend herself against a herd of animals made from crystal. She tried to quiet her breathing, but she still panted heavily after running.

Sniffing at the air once more, one deer ventured on its delicate feet below the bridge, coming within inches of Zuri.

Shaking in fear, she shrank away from the creature.

But the deer paid no attention to her. Instead, it pawed at the ground and then walked under the bridge to the grass on the other side. The rest of the herd followed, and her discarded contacts crunched under their feet.

Zuri wondered if the destruction of her Personal Bubble had anything to do with the reason why the deer ignored her. Proceeding with caution, she followed them out from under the bridge. She looked up at the streetlamps lining the sidewalk winding through the Carnival of Animals.

All streetlamps had reassumed their default position. Each lamp head looked down at the sidewalk, oblivious to Zuri's presence.

Before she realized it, the angry mob rounded a corner a short distance away.

Zuri ran in the opposite direction, toward the harbor.

"I see something!" a man in the crowd shouted. "Running that way!"

The mob rushed after Zuri.

Still winded from sprinting into the Carnival of Animals, Zuri struggled to keep moving but her legs failed her. When she saw a crystal peacock strut nearby, Zuri used her remaining energy to step off the sidewalk and roll in the grass toward it. Desperate, she tried to hide behind it.

Dozens of men and women jogged past the point where Zuri had left the sidewalk, slowing to a stop and looking all around the park. Others lagged behind.

"Where did she go?" a matronly woman said. "How did she get away?"

"I don't know," the young man who had spotted Zuri moments ago said. "But she's got to be here somewhere."

When the peacock strutting between Zuri and the mob cried out loudly and fanned its tail open, Zuri stifled a scream, convinced her presence would become obvious.

Everyone looked at the peacock. Within seconds, they all looked away from it, still searching the grounds for Zuri.

Zuri came to a quick realization.

They're all inside their Personal Bubbles. I destroyed my Personal Bubble. That means my virtual presence no longer exists. They can't see any sign of the virtual me. The real world—the real me—is muted. I'm in their background.

She thought about the man who had led the crowd because he claimed to see Zuri running.

When I ran, he probably saw some kind of blur in the background.

I don't have a virtual presence anymore, and that's all they can see.

None of them can see what's real.

None of them can see what's staring them in the face.

Emboldened by her thoughts and desperate to live, Zuri crawled slowly from behind the peacock, staying on the grass and keeping silent.

The matron spoke up. "I heard something." She paused, reminding Zuri of the way the herd of deer had sniffed the air around Benjamin.

A teenage girl raised her hand. "I found a way to bring up her PDA. I'll put him on Speaker."

"Oh, my word," Benjamin's voice said. "Where am I? Who are you?"

Zuri froze in place, terrified that Benjamin would point her out to them.

How can he? Benjamin exists in connecting space, not in the real world. Even if they've hacked into him, how could he see me when we're not in the same place?

Hoping her logic would hold, Zuri stood up while everyone in the mob turned to face the teenage girl.

"Where is Zuri?" the teenager said.

Taking slow steps to avoid creating a blur of motion, Zuri walked across the grass toward the sidewalk beyond the horde of incensed people.

"I'm sure I don't know." Benjamin's disembodied voice floated through the air. "Miss Zuri has vanished. I can't find her anywhere."

Zuri aimed one foot toward the sidewalk but then thought better of it, remembering how she'd heard the clatter of hoof steps against it when the herd of deer crossed it. Instead, she kept to the grass but followed the path of the sidewalk toward the harbor.

The Animated Garden full of vibrant and inquisitive flowers loomed ahead with the water garden beyond. If she could make it to the water garden, maybe the mob wouldn't think to go that far to look for her. Maybe they would assume she'd head back into the city.

The teenage girl wielded a sharp knife and spoke to Benjamin. "Tell me where she is so I can slice her throat." The girl paused. "If you don't, I know how to snuff you out of existence. All it takes is a few keystrokes."

Zuri fought the fierce urge to bolt. She turned her back on the mob and continued her slow and steady pace.

"Truly, I don't know!" Benjamin cried.

A sizzling sound cracked through the air.

"Well, he was useless," the teen said.

The water park grew closer. Just a few steps ahead, the sidewalk in the Carnival of Animals led into the Animated Garden. Beyond it, Zuri could see where the garden's sidewalk turned into a marble walkway flanked by sparkling clean canals stretching in all directions. Alongside the canals, dozens of fountains sprayed streams of water in time to distant music.

Behind, the man who had first seen Zuri said, "If she's here, there's a reason we can't see her. Maybe she's outside her bubble. We should take ours off."

Hoping she'd put enough distance between herself and the throng behind her, Zuri dashed through the Animated Garden and then into the water garden, hurrying toward the harbor.

"I see her!" the man shouted. "She's going into the water garden!"

With cries of rage, the mass of people swarmed after Zuri.

Catching sight of the harbor ahead, Zuri's heart sank when she saw no one there.

But how could anyone be there to help her? Benjamin had promised to help only to become useless.

Now what?

Frantic to save herself, Zuri darted off the path to hide behind a fountain.

"There!" the matronly woman yelled, running with the assurance of a marathoner despite her age. "She's by that fountain! We've got her cornered."

Zuri considered her options.

Canals and fountains flanked the sidewalk. She saw nowhere else to run.

She remembered Karen and that shark that had leapt out of the canal near the bridge in the Carnival of Animals.

Sometimes sharks come out of the ocean and into the canals.

Zuri saw a solution. She stepped inside a large fountain shaped like a crescent moon and sank into its water, only two feet deep. The fountain shot a steady fan of water that waved back and forth.

"Somewhere around here," the matron shouted, pulling up alongside Zuri's fountain. "Spread out. She can't hide forever."

But after failing to locate Zuri, the mass of people shifted deeper into the water garden and then back toward the Carnival of Animals, fuming and baffled by her disappearance.

Still inside the fountain, Zuri remained

between narrow rows of underwater pipes, still clinging to them to make sure she stayed underwater. Periodically, she lifted her nose just far enough above the water's surface to take a deep breath. Hearing an absence of voices, Zuri raised her head high enough, still camouflaged by the water streaming from the pipes, to take account of the situation.

Everyone else had vanished.

Zuri climbed out of the fountain and ran as fast as she could to the harbor. Not knowing what else to do, she rushed toward the bullseye where she first had landed. As she stepped onto the bullseye, Zuri looked up at the sound of a drone taxi and saw its rollercoaster harness reaching down toward her.

Uncertainty seized her. She shivered, her drenched clothes clinging tightly to her skin.

What if it's a trap? What if that mob sent it?

Unlike the singleton drone that had brought her to VainGlory, this taxi was a two-seater, and a dark figure sat in the other seat.

Zuri gathered her wits, ready to run away. She could run to the Welcome Center and hide inside. She could run back to the water garden and hide in a different fountain.

The taxi lowered and tilted so she could

see who sat in the other seat.

"Come on, Zuri. Get in!" The man extended one hand to her, even though she wouldn't be able to reach it unless she allowed the unfurling rollercoaster harness to embrace her.

Startled by the sight of his pale green eyes, Zuri muttered, "Ben?"

Maybe he read her lips, because the noise of the drone must have drowned out her whisper. "It's me. Rameen. Your brother." His brow creased in apprehension. "If you don't come with me right now, they're going to kill you!"

Memories rushed back. The way her parents ignored her or misunderstood her. The way her parents paid more attention to their devices and their screens than they did to their children. And the one person who genuinely cared about her.

Rameen.

Zuri opened her arms to the drone taxi's grip and let it pull her up inside the cab, where Rameen hugged her close as the vehicle sped high into the air and away from the shores of VainGlory.

CHAPTER 29

Once the drone taxi landed at the airport on the nearby independent island of Reclaim and they walked far enough away to hear each other speak over the chopping blades, Zuri said, "What are you doing here? How did you find me? Are you taking me back to Aspire?"

"No." Rameen led Zuri away from the drone taxi and toward a small plane. "It isn't safe to talk yet. We have to get out of here. I need you to trust me. Can you do that?"

Other than Mae Lin, the only other person Zuri had ever truly trusted was her brother. "Of course," she said.

A few hours later, their plane landed in the last place Zuri ever wanted to see again. Ten years ago, she'd made her way to Aspire and never looked back. She became tight-lipped as Rameen took her to a car and drove her home. Zuri stared straight ahead in anger, although she couldn't help but notice how a lush greenness seemed to press against the roads. Other than the pavement, trees and bushes and grasses appeared to be taking over the world.

"I guess you have a lot of questions," Rameen said.

Zuri could tell that he glanced at her, but she kept her eyes focused ahead and her mouth shut.

"We've been trying to find you since you left," Rameen said. He took one hand off the steering wheel and snapped his fingers. "Vanished without a trace. Even I couldn't find you, and I was a pretty good hacker, even back then. Of course, I was looking for your real name, not one you made up." He grunted in disgust. "Blacksheep. Really, Zuri? You changed your name to Blacksheep."

"It seemed appropriate," Zuri grumbled.

"I would have found you faster if you'd gone by 'Zuri Blacksheep' instead of just 'Blacksheep.' That's the one thing I have to give credit to VainGlory for—they wouldn't take you in until you gave them your first name. Once that got into their database, I found you."

Zuri couldn't help but raise an eyebrow in surprise. "You hacked into VainGlory? I thought the city was supposed to be unhackable."

"Yeah, well, I made sure I got a lot of practice before you arrived in VainGlory."

They sat in silence for several minutes.

"Were you Ben?" Zuri said. "Did you hack into my Personal Digital Assistant?"

Rameen raised his voice in protest. "And changed his eyes from yellow to green. Honestly, Zuri how could you not know it was me? Why do think I changed the color of his eyes?"

"You haven't been around for ten years. Why would I expect you to show up now?"

"Because you were in danger!" Rameen blurted. Gathering his emotions, he lowered his voice. "I haven't been around because you left and no one could find you. Until now."

Zuri mulled over his words, growing more confused by the moment. "But you hacked into Ben the same day I arrived in VainGlory. Those people didn't turn against me until today. How did you know they were going to do it?"

"I didn't."

"But you knew I was in danger."

Rameen pulled the car into the driveway of an old saltbox house with fading cornflower blue paint. The house where they'd grown up. "You might have heard that things are different now. Welcome to Middlesex Province. Welcome to the Northeast Kingdom."

CHAPTER 30

Inside her family home, Zuri sank deeper into reluctance. Knowing she couldn't have remained in VainGlory without being lynched, she considered being here the next worse thing.

The way her parents had aged surprise-ed Zuri. Although they'd been detached and distant, Zuri remembered them as seeming young and vibrant. Now, their faces looked weathered, and gray streaked their hair.

While Zuri squirmed in an armchair, Rameen sat on the floor nearby, and her parents perched on the edge of a sofa.

"We know we screwed up," her father said. "We never meant to do it, but it happened. We didn't realize how we hurt you and your brother. Not until you left."

"I knew you were alive," her mother said in a choked voice. "I never gave up."

Zuri squirmed. "I'm surprised you noticed I wasn't there."

Her father's face sagged in sorrow. "I didn't realize how I'd lost touch with the actual world until it was too late. Not until you were gone."

"We learned," her mother said in a voice gaining strength. "When you left, the shock of it shook us out of that dream-like state we'd fallen into. Discovering you had vanished, not knowing where you were, and trying to find you—it changed everything." She gripped her husband's hand.

Zuri rolled her eyes. "So, you live in the Kingdom now."

"Don't laugh," Rameen said. "Mom's a chieftain."

Zuri groaned in disbelief.

"Actually," her mother said. "Your brother's telling the truth. Your father and I were like lotus eaters, oblivious to the world. You're the one who shook us out of that malaise. When I say we've changed, I'm serious."

"Fine," Zuri said. "But I don't want to be here. Anywhere but here."

"You know that's not going to happen," Rameen said.

Zuri bristled.

"Not yet," her father amended. "You were born in Middlesex Province, and that makes you a native of the Kingdom. You can live anywhere you want." He paused.

"After you complete rehab."

Zuri thought she must have misunderstood. "Did you say rehab? As in rehabilitation?"

"As in junkie," Rameen said.

Zuri laughed. "You know better. I don't drink. I don't smoke. I stay away from drugs, even when they're over the counter."

"We know," her mother said.

Zuri scrunched up her face in revulsion. "Then why is my brother calling me a junkie?"

"You wore Slim Goggles for years," Rameen said. "Then you went to VainGlory and entered a Personal Bubble."

"So?" Zuri said. "That's what everyone does." She shot a pointed look at her parents. "You should know that better than anyone else."

"We do," her father said in compassion. "It's why we recognize the signs."

"It's going to be hard during the next few days," her mother said. "The next few weeks. The next few months. But no matter how bad it gets you'll be surrounded by people who care about you. People who love you. People who want you to get better."

Deciding she'd had enough, Zuri left the room in a huff and opened the front door, determined to leave. She'd struck out on her own before. She could do it again.

A large man stood outside, blocking the doorway.

"You have got to be kidding," Zuri said.

The moment Zuri set foot outside, the man grabbed her wrist, snapped a blinking device around it, and locked it in place next to the bracelet she still wore. The diamonds in that bracelet sparkled with every blink.

Although the device weighed no more than a pound, its presence around her wrist made Zuri feel like a trapped animal. "Get this off!" she yelled at the man.

Instead of paying attention to her, the man waved at her family inside the house and then walked away.

Looking up, Zuri saw her parents standing on the threshold.

"It's a tracking device," her father said. "Wherever you go, we'll know where you are. If you step within 20 miles of any border of the Kingdom, all border stations will be alerted automatically. For your own good, you won't be allowed to leave."

Zuri scrunched her fingers together and tried to push the device over her hand, but it wouldn't budge. "What's wrong with you people? I'm not a criminal! Let me go!"

Zuri wished she had never left Aspire. Despite the struggle, she'd been happy working with Mae Lin. The work they did together made Zuri proud and happy. She'd had a good life in Aspire.

Why did everything have to fall apart because she went to VainGlory?

Zuri had felt endangered when she left

the city. For the first time, she considered the possibility that it might have been a misunderstanding. Something that could be explained. Maybe even fixed. Everything else in VainGlory had been perfect. What if it could be perfect again?

Zuri sank to the ground, sobbing in grief for all she had lost.

Her mother knelt next to Zuri and spoke in a soft voice. "When you lived in Aspire and VainGlory, you thought you were connected to the world. You weren't. You were connected to an illusion. You thought you were a businesswoman selling a product. You weren't. You *are* the product. All those places care about is collecting information about you. All they want is to use you."

"No!" Zuri cried, squeezing her hands over her ears. "Leave me alone!"

When Rameen spoke, his voice sounded muffled, but Zuri understood his words. "It's too soon. She's not ready to hear the truth yet."

Still weeping, Zuri wrapped her arms around her head in a desperate attempt to keep all of them out, forgetting the mob that had chased her through VainGlory and desperate to go back.

CHAPTER 31

Days later, Zuri woke up to the sound of her bedroom door banging open.

"Get up," a man's voice said.

Startled, Zuri clutched the covers against her as she sat up. Squinting against the startling light of day that streamed through the flowery curtains covering the windows, she stared at an unfamiliar dark shape in the doorway. "Who are you? Where's Janice?"

"Gone," the man said. "Transferred to Degeneration Hall." He paused. "You don't want to go there. It's like a prison. Be smart, get up, get dressed, eat your breakfast before it gets cold." Without another word, he stepped into the hallway and shut her bedroom door behind him.

"I'm already in a prison," Zuri muttered. She rolled over and pulled the covers over her head. She didn't want to get up. She didn't want to get dressed or eat breakfast. All she had the energy to do was curl up in a fetal position and feel sorry for herself.

When she thought about VainGlory, she hyperventilated.

I had everything in VainGlory. And now I'm left out. What if they've forgotten about me? What if Milan is wondering where I am? What is Donna thinking about me?

The sensation of being left out—of feeling invisible—made Zuri frantic with anxiety. And yet she couldn't force her body to move.

A loud pounding on her door shook Zuri out of her thoughts.

"Now!" the man's voice shouted.

What if I'm sent to that place where Janice went? What if they lock people inside?

Unable to bear the idea of things becoming worse, Zuri forced herself out of bed and into a pair of jeans and a long-sleeved shirt. She dragged her body out of the bedroom and into the community kitchen of the Recovery House, an old farmhouse with simple furnishings.

A man with a hawkish nose and his black hair in a buzz cut stood at the stove and scrambled eggs in a cast iron skillet. He looked young, maybe Zuri's age. Focused on the skillet, he said, "Coffee's on the table."

Zuri sat at a roughly-hewn wooden table, picked up a blue-speckled mug filled with steaming black coffee, and took small sips. Still unused to the harsh appearance and sensation of the world she'd left ten years ago, Zuri tried to stay calm by staring at the coffee.

The man dropped a plate full of eggs in front of her. "Eat." He took a fork out of a glass vase holding cutlery and shoved it across the table at Zuri until it clinked against her plate.

Zuri jumped and let go of her mug in surprise.

The man snatched the mug before it could tip over, swearing when the steaming coffee splashed against his skin. Without another word, he wiped up the spilled liquid and put the mug next to Zuri's plate. "Eat."

Too afraid to do anything else, Zuri obeyed but stared at her plate. She shuddered when she heard him sit opposite her. Glancing up, she saw him eat from his own plate of eggs. Before she could think better of it, she said, "Who are you?"

The young man looked up at her with black eyes. "John Running Horse."

Zuri shifted her concentration back to her own breakfast. She couldn't think of anything else to say.

They ate in silence.

Finally, John finished, took his plate, fork, and empty mug to the sink where he washed, dried, and put them away. As he walked out the front door, John said, "Clean up after yourself before you come outside."

Unused to eating with anything she didn't throw away afterwards, it took some time for Zuri to learn how to clean everything, grateful she'd managed to sneak a glance at John when he'd been at the sink.

Zuri wanted to crawl back into bed. She felt drained and used up after the simple task of eating breakfast and its aftermath.

She'd heard of Natives before, but she'd never seen one in VainGlory or even Aspire. She'd never even met one before leaving home. Zuri wondered if her ignorance could hurt his feelings, and she didn't want to face him.

But she dreaded being sent to a house with stricter rules more than she feared facing John.

Zuri eased her way outside and walked around the house to the wide expanse of yard that had been churned up. The briny smell from several open bags of raw fish threatened to knock her unconscious.

John shoveled fish out of one bag and onto the ground next to it.

Zuri approached him, keeping her gaze on the ground while avoiding the fish.

John continued shoveling. "How long were you connected?"

When the fish he shoveled landed close

to Zuri's feet, she took a hurried step back. "Ten years in Aspire. Then several weeks in VainGlory."

"I hear it's worse in VainGlory."

Zuri didn't understand what he meant. "It's better," she mumbled. "Slim Goggles make you feel immersed in the connection. But in VainGlory you get a Personal Bubble. It's like you *are* the connection."

"Like I said," John said in a dispassionate voice. "It's worse in VainGlory."

He continued shoveling, and Zuri stood by him, waiting. After several minutes, she said, "This is supposed to be my first day of work."

"So, work."

"I don't know what to do."

With a thud, John drove his shovel into upturned earth. "You never done this before?"

Zuri shook her head, still concentrating on the ground. She didn't understand why the fish had died or why John wanted to bury them here. It seemed to Zuri that even dead fish belonged in the sea.

"Then pay attention to everything I say and watch what I do."

When John said nothing more, Zuri dared to glance up, startled by the intense way he stared at her.

"Do you understand what we're doing?" he said.

Looking down again, Zuri shook her

head.

"Do you know what this is? Where we're standing?"

Zuri mumbled, "In the back yard?"

"First, we use fish to fertilize the earth and provide nutrients. Then we plant. Kale. Chard. Lettuce. Beans. Broccoli. And more. Understand?"

Zuri gave a weak shrug.

"This," John said, "is where food comes from."

Zuri looked up, failing to hide the surprise on her face.

John's voice softened. "Maybe your food came to you in boxes before. Maybe it appeared out of nowhere, like magic. But this is the real magic. We plant seeds, tend to the plants that grow from them, nourish them. The plants provide food, nourish us."

Zuri realized that she'd never thought about where food came from until this moment. John was right: food had always appeared in boxes, seemingly out of nowhere. She'd never considered how food got into boxes.

"You'll need this." John pushed the wooden handle of his shovel into her hands, his fingers lingering against hers.

Zuri couldn't help but look down at them. Unlike Shepard Green's perfect skin, John's looked dirty and rough. Unlike Shepard Green's manicured nails, John's looked unkempt. Unlike Shepard Green's scent of pine, John reeked of sweat.

Zuri didn't want to show her repugnance. With all her might, she willed herself to stand firm instead of stepping away in horror at his lack of proper grooming.

For the rest of the day, Zuri learned how to prepare and plant the garden. She followed John's lead and copied everything he did.

By the end of the day, Zuri couldn't help but notice the dirt under her own nails and the shocking stench of what appeared to be her own sweat.

She rushed into the shower inside and scrubbed frantically to rid herself of the dirt and the stench.

When Zuri went to bed that night, she thought about her plan before falling asleep. More and more, she believed her exit from VainGlory had happened because of some kind of strange mistake or misunderstanding. Her previous companion and fellow housemate Janice had shared not only her plan to escape with Zuri. Janice had also found a spare key card, which Zuri kept hidden under her mattress.

Now that Janice had been sent to Degeneration Hall, Zuri realized Janice couldn't guide her anymore. It was up to Zuri to decide when to use that key card.

CHAPTER 32

Zuri wanted to run away and hide.

Standing in a crowd of dozens of people of all ages, Zuri felt smothered and trapped. While she'd been enamored of the hundreds of icons that had jammed around her in VainGlory, they hadn't been able to touch her, even if that meant little more than brushing lightly against her. More important, Zuri had been in control. She had the power to dismiss icons any time she wanted or simply mute them.

She had no power to mute the people standing all around her, much less get rid of them with the wave of her hand.

How can people live like this?

Zuri kept her arms wrapped tightly around her torso like armor. As always, she kept her gaze on the ground in an effort to shut out the sight of the crowd.

Unfortunately, she couldn't muffle their voices.

Standing beside her—monitoring her—John had explained that tonight's event was called a lecture. Despite his clarification that one person would speak and all others would listen, Zuri saw no point in such a thing.

Even worse, Zuri wondered if the lecture was aimed at her.

A middle-aged woman stood at the front of a large hall, and most of the crowd sat on simple benches lined in rows facing her. Zuri stood at the back with John and others who arrived too late to find an empty seat. The woman said, "Almost everyone has a perfectly good brain. What I'm here to discuss is why we must pay attention to what we expose our brains to."

Zuri despaired in waves of homesickness for the life she'd left behind. She missed her wall of icons. She missed her friends.

"While technology benefits our lives," the woman continued, "it also has the power to diminish our brains. And when our brains are diminished, each one of us becomes far less than what we have the power to be. Instead of being fully fleshed-out human beings, we become the equivalent of paper dolls. Our thinking becomes superficial and simplistic."

When Zuri scoffed, John gave her a hard nudge.

"You know I have a love-hate relationship with technology," the woman said with a smile.

Everyone in the room except for Zuri and John laughed. But when Zuri peeked at him, she saw one corner of John's mouth turn up.

"I don't have to tell you about all the ways technology helps our province and the entire Kingdom," the woman said. "But it has a darker side. If we depend too much on it, we fail to encourage our brains to work. If we spend too much time with it, addiction can be triggered. And then there is the matter of manipulation."

Zuri closed her eyes and drummed up the memory of her home in the Platinum Tower. She remembered how her meals were delivered. She remembered Benjamin—the one with yellow eyes, before her brother Rameen infiltrated and took over her Personal Digital Assistant.

The woman paced across the platform on which she stood. "It can be difficult to tell when people have taken over any given channel of connection. People with agendas. People who stand to benefit if they succeed in manipulating us. But by questioning the source of information on these channels—by coming to lectures like this one or even having face-to-face conversations with others in the community—we can keep our critical thinking intact. We can keep our brains healthy and active. We can avoid becoming paper dolls."

Zuri remembered the first day she'd arrived in VainGlory. Now, she thought of it as the best day of her life. That night, she'd presented Mae Lin's work in the Carnival of Animals and then saved Karen's life when the shark attacked her. Zuri remembered how people had admired her, how they'd loved her.

A lanky man with graying hair stood from one of the benches and spoke. "Old habits die hard. Sometimes I can't help but go back to sites where I can talk to my friends. Friends I've known all my life. Some days it goes well, and everything stays civil." The man paused and rubbed his head as if someone had clocked him. "But sooner or later one of them says something stupid, and I can't help but call them out. Then they say something even more stupid. These people matter to me. I care about them. I don't want to lose them. What do I do?"

The woman faced him and folded her hands together. "I think we all face that problem. Remember this: when your friends say something that makes no sense to you, they are probably reacting to something they've seen or heard with pure emotion. Odds are they've become so entrenched with the sites they love that their perfectly good brains no longer function at more than a superficial level. Your friends have lost their ability for critical thinking. They don't realize that their emotions aren't the same as facts. They think information is knowledge, but they've lost the ability to *turn* information into knowledge. They might as well be children lost in the woods who are convinced they know where they are and how to get out."

Zuri remembered how she'd created the maze and its resounding success. She thought about all the endorsements she'd received and the breaking trends that made her famous.

"I get that," the lanky man said. "But how do I talk to them? How do I help them?"

The woman's voice sobered. "I don't think you can. Not unless they come to a place like the Kingdom."

The lanky man's voice cracked with pain. "But I care about them."

"I know," the woman said. "But just because they're acting like children doesn't mean they are children. They're adults. They're responsible for their own actions and decisions, just like each of us is responsible for our actions and decisions."

Zuri perked up at those words.

I'm responsible for my actions and decisions. Just because I'm here doesn't mean I have to stay here. I can decide to go back to VainGlory. I can decide to stay there.

"It's a new kind of war we're fighting,"

the woman continued. "And what each of us can do is resist the temptation to get involved with paper dolls who have stopped using their perfectly good brains. I'm not saying you should give up on your friends, but think of them as magpies who are distracted by every shiny thing without taking the time to think about what that shiny thing is or means or if it can harm them."

When everyone applauded, Zuri joined with enthusiasm, because the people who were trying to dissuade her had unwittingly encouraged her to find a way back to Vain-Glory.

CHAPTER 33

The next day, Zuri concentrated on acting the way she suspected John Running Horse wanted her to behave. She worked hard in the garden, paying attention and following orders. When John asked what she thought of last night's lecture, Zuri told him she felt inspired by it. She even forced herself to ask John a few questions and learned he'd earned a degree in agriculture in a province located 100 miles to the west.

Zuri hid her discomfort, even though every moment she spent in the harsh and all-too-real presence of another person made her want to scream. Last night, surrounded by hundreds of people she didn't know, Zuri had never felt lonelier. The world around her seemed strange and uncertain. Fear seeped into her bones and filled them like marrow.

Once night fell, Zuri ate an early dinner and claimed to be exhausted from the day's work. Alone in the bedroom she'd previously shared with Janice, Zuri went through all of her former housemate's secret hiding places, relieved to find the treasures Janice had concealed. A flashlight under a loose floorboard. An open-ended train ticket pushed to the back of a high shelf in the closet. A forged document on a slip of yellow paper that would allow her to enter VainGlory without question.

Keeping the lights off and the bedroom in the dark, Zuri stayed under the covers, hiding the fresh set of clothes she wore in case John should find a reason to bother her.

Finally, when the crack under the bedroom door showed the house had gone dark—meaning John had retired to his own room for the night—Zuri retrieved all her treasures, including the key card hidden under the mattress. Knowing the floorboards outside her room would creak and alert John if she tried to walk out the front door, Zuri opened one of the large bedroom windows, eased her way through it, and hopped onto the soft grass outside.

Moonlight lit up the complex in which the Recovery House stood. Once a village run by the fishing industry, dozens of houses ranging from salt boxes to colonials stood on either side of the Recovery House. The houses jammed close together, a remnant of fishermen needing no yards because they spent most of their time at sea. All of the houses faced the expansive open greenery of the town common. A white bandstand gleamed in the heart of the common, and sidewalks lined with iron streetlamps emitting yellow beams of light crossed its lush grounds like a lattice.

Glancing around, Zuri saw only a man walking a dog a few blocks down the street. Hoping he wouldn't notice her, she strolled toward the common and entered through one of its decorative iron gates. Although she stepped softly, Zuri's footsteps sounded too loud. She held her breath until she had crossed the common and faced a grand house on its opposite side.

Satisfied that the house stood dark, Zuri remembered what Janice had told her.

It's where they keep all the technology for connecting with the rest of the world. No one lives there, but they keep it locked up. We can get in with the key card, get connected, and line up everything we need to get out of here.

Janice had warned they should avoid the front door, because she'd spotted security cameras on the porch.

Zuri circled around the side of the house and discovered what appeared to be an entrance to a mud room. Not wanting to draw attention from the house next door, which stood close enough to block the moonlight, Zuri noticed a tiny dot of red light next to the mudroom door.

The key pad.

She held the key card against it, grateful when the dot of red light changed to green in silence, instead of beeping loudly like many key pads. Zuri opened the door and slipped inside, listening for the click to make sure the door had latched shut.

Safely inside, Zuri turned on the flashlight, keeping its beam on the floor to avoid detection from outside. Finding nothing on the main floor, Zuri winced when she climbed the groaning stairway to the floor above. She soon found a windowless room and dared to turn on the lights.

A wall filled with screens came to life, along with the keypad gloves scattered on the long table beneath them.

Next to the keypad gloves stood a box filled with Slim Goggles.

Zuri's heart raced with joy. Her fear and discomfort melted away at the sight of everything that had been so cruelly stripped away from her.

Not caring about the fit, Zuri grabbed the first pair of Slim Goggles and gloves, jamming them onto her body.

The cruelty of the world vanished, replaced by brighter and prettier sites. Unlike the wall of icons she'd experienced inside her Personal Bubble in VainGlory, everything she wanted was displayed on the screens in front of her, reminding her of the reality of the room in which she stood.

Still, compared to her nightmarish existence since arriving in the Middlesex Province, this poor excuse of using Slim Goggles felt like ecstasy.

Opening up to a sense of floating in a state of comfort and pleasure, Zuri sank into the world now allowed by the Slim Goggles, sinking into the welcome sense of being surrounded by all the sites she knew and loved. Even though Zuri didn't dare log into any of them for fear that her family would trace her steps, this superficial access would provide all the details she'd need to escape.

A banner-like ribbon announcement displayed across all screens.

Exciting news from VainGlory!

Adrenaline surged through Zuri's body. Desperate to know what that news promised, she reached out with her gloved hand and clicked on the banner.

One screen filled with a clip of Zuri with wrists handcuffed behind her back being led by a group of armed guards into an ornate marble building. An engraved sign above the front door read "Highest Judicial Court of VainGlory."

Startled by the sight, Zuri pulled up a chair and sat down in front of the screen.

"That never happened. No one arrested me."

News bubbles popped into view around the handcuffed Zuri, each announcing its own commentary. Although the newscasters talked over each other, Zuri could pick out some snippets.

"After being convicted of the murder of Shepard Green..."

"... expected to receive a sentence ... "

"Zuri Blacksheep now faces what could be a death..."

"... showed no remorse at the verdict ..."

"... considered to be a psychopath although not diagnosed by ..."

"Psychopath?" Zuri said out loud. She leaned closer to the screen. "Why are they talking about me? That can't be me."

And yet, every news clip showcased Zuri—not an obvious imposter, but someone who looked and sounded exactly like Zuri. "This is impossible. None of this ever happened. How can they be reporting it?"

"A better question is what do they have to gain?"

Zuri jerked her head up. Past the thin veneer of the world her Slim Goggles displayed, Zuri saw Rameen standing in the doorway alongside John Running Horse.

Her first instinct was to run, but both men blocked the only path out of the room. The fear of getting caught paralyzed her briefly, soon replaced by indignation.

Too late, Zuri noticed the rapidly flashing lights on the tracking band locked around her wrist. She'd assumed that waiting until late at night meant everyone would sleep through any alerts they might receive from the tracker. Apparently, she'd guessed wrong.

"Fine," Zuri said, still sitting in front of the screen showing footage of her being escorted through the lofty halls of the courtroom in VainGlory. She gestured toward the screen. "What do they have to gain by this?" Before either man could answer, a new possibility occurred to Zuri. Standing with increasing indignation, she pointed an accusing finger at Rameen. "You did this!"

Rameen remained calm. "I did not."

Zuri fumed. "How am I supposed to believe that? You hacked into VainGlory. You broke into my Personal Bubble disguised as my Personal Digital Assistant. You've already manipulated me. Fooled me." She flipped her hands up in the air. "This is just one of your tricks."

"It's no trick," Rameen said. "What you're seeing is why I hacked into VainGlory. It's why I came to save you."

Zuri choked out a laugh. "Save me? From what?"

"Let me show you."

Zuri swept one arm in a grand gesture. "Be my guest."

When Rameen entered the room, John

shifted to center his body in the doorway to block any hope that Zuri could get past him.

She took a step back when Rameen sat in the chair she'd abandoned.

Rameen focused his attention on a smaller screen next to the one showing Zuri in the courthouse as he donned a pair of keypad gloves. Navigating through a set of dialog boxes on the smaller screen, he entered a program that played back a recording that Zuri recognized at once.

"Do you remember," Rameen said, centering and enlarging the recording, "the day we went into your storage space and found a locked door and a locked trunk behind it?"

Rameen waved one hand, and an image of the steamer trunk they'd found hovered in the air.

Zuri nodded, forgetting she stood behind her brother where he couldn't see her. She remembered how along with the green-eyed Benjamin—who she now understood had been Rameen—she'd succeeded in opening the locked door but neither had found a way to open the box, which appeared to be an old-fashioned trunk that people used hundreds of years ago. "There was a label on it. With my name."

"Yes." Rameen glanced over his shoulder at her. "Do you remember who the box was addressed to?"

Zuri frowned. She remembered because it still struck her as odd. "Franklin Buckingham." The inventor of the Personal Bubble and the owner of the company that manufactured it. "What does that have to do with anything?"

"It took a while, but I can open it now." Without waiting for Zuri to respond, Rameen tapped his fingers in the air, which resulted in the trunk's lock changing color from gray to amber to green.

The lock popped open.

With a swift gesture, Rameen waved the trunk lid open. When an audio track displayed on the screen, he advanced the bar to the halfway point and then let it play.

A document floated out of the trunk, and a disembodied voice said, "... may reside in any residence earned in VainGlory as long as you comply with the laws of the city."

In that audio recording, Zuri's voice said, "Yes."

"What?" Zuri said. "That's my voice. What is my voice doing there? I never agreed to anything like that." She paused. "What exactly is that?"

Rameen gestured toward the smaller screen, where the audio continued. "... with the understanding that a failure of compliance results in the loss of all rights."

Again, in the audio, Zuri's voice said, "Yes."

Rameen paused the audio and waved up more materials out of the trunk displayed on the screen. "There's a medical report for Franklin Buckingham. The other one is a report of your DNA."

Zuri stepped forward. Placing both hands on the table, she leaned so close to the smaller screen that she had to ease back to regain her focus on it. "Heart failure," she read from the medical report. "This says he needs a transplant." She shifted her gaze to her own DNA report, which had been stamped with one word.

Match.

Her head swam until Zuri thought she would pass out. Bracing her hands against the table, she kept staring at the screen but said, "You want me to think Franklin Buckingham wanted my heart to replace his? That's ridiculous. He'd never leave this kind of evidence in my storage space."

"We think it's for legal reasons," John said, still blocking the doorway. "When you found it, the trunk was locked. Even with Rameen's help, you couldn't get it open. But they can prove the documents were there and have your voice proving you agreed to their terms."

Zuri considered what she'd just heard. "But all my voice says is 'yes.' They could have recorded me saying that any time." Her thoughts shifted. "But the locked box proves I didn't have access to what's inside.

It proves I didn't know anything about it. It proves they manipulated me."

"Just because everything was locked when we found it," Rameen said, "doesn't mean they didn't unlock everything as soon as you left VainGlory." He gestured toward the larger screen, now showing Zuri standing before a judge in a courtroom. "They were going to kill you so Franklin Buckingham could take your heart. They're covering up your escape. This is how they're doing it."

One of the news bubbles shouted, "Death by hanging!"

Another banner crossed all screens, announcing, "Public hanging scheduled tomorrow at Noon. Stay tuned!"

Doubt nagged at Zuri. "Or maybe you're making all this up. Maybe you're the one who's trying to manipulate me."

"I'm not," Rameen insisted.

"Prove it." Zuri became emboldened. "Take me back to VainGlory so I can see for myself. It's a public hanging, right? Let's go watch."

"It's too dangerous," John said. "Rameen says Buckingham hasn't found a replacement heart yet. If anyone sees you, you might as well be dead."

"I hacked in once," Rameen said. "I can do it again. Everyone in VainGlory is so wrapped up in their own little world that no one will notice us. We can get in, and we won't be inside a Personal Bubble. Not even Slim Goggles. We'll walk in the real world. We'll be in plain sight, and we'll be invisible."

"But her mosaic," John said. "It's embedded in her identity chip. VainGlory is lousy with surveillance cameras—they'll recognize her mosaic. What if it's not just surveillance cameras? Recognition devices could be everywhere."

"Easy," Rameen said. "We'll take out her identity chip and replace it with somebody else's."

Zuri rubbed the fleshy part of her thumb, feeling the hard edge of the identity chip beneath it. "No. If you take it out, it'll wipe out my mosaic."

"Yeah," Rameen said. "So?"

"You're forgetting where she came from," John said. "You're forgetting what it's done to her."

Zuri backed away, ready to fight back if they tried to pry the chip out of her hand. "You're not getting my mosaic! I can't lose it. It's my life!"

She remembered how Milan had explained the mosaic to her.

It's everything I buy. Everything I want. Everything I consider. Each individual thing is like a tile in a mosaic. Everyone has hundreds of thousands of tiles in their mosaic. My mosaic is who I am. Without it, I'd be nothing.

"A mosaic is nothing more than data," Rameen protested. "It's just a way for companies to target you for selling their products to you."

"But that's me," Zuri said. She kept backing away until a wall stopped her. "All of those tiles in my mosaic. They define me. They create me. They're what make me *me*."

Rameen leaned back in his chair and stared at her. "God, Zuri. What have they done to you?"

John took a careful step into the room. "You're not made up of things," he said. "Sure, you've got a mosaic. But the tiles in your mosaic are made up of experiences. Decisions you've made. The woman you've chosen to become."

His words made no sense. "But that's all the same thing," Zuri said. "It's the same as all the things I want. What I have." Her voice choked with emotion. "What I had before you took me from VainGlory." Tears fell down her face. "Before you took away everything I spent my whole life working for!"

Rameen perked up. "That's not what John means."

John pointed at the bank of screens and said, "Show her."

Rameen's gloved hands wiped away the display from all screens except the one showing Zuri being led out of the courtroom and through a jeering crowd.

One screen filled with the image of a very young Zuri catching first sight of a large egg in a field of hay bales and children scampering among them. The young Zuri's face brightened as she trotted forward only to pull up short when she noticed an even younger child toddling toward it. Smiling, the young Zuri held back, happily watching the toddler approach the large egg, on the verge of winning the hunt.

"That's just one tile in your mosaic," Rameen said. "It shows how you're kind and generous. Here's another one."

A different screen showed the same image from another angle, its audio track filled with whispers from her parents—oblivious to the fact that Zuri stood still—telling their daughter to let the toddler win.

"You're right," Rameen said. "They didn't see you. They didn't give you credit for who you are. But your mosaic does." He brought up another screen.

The new image showed the same egg hunt where a young Rameen shouted at his parents while wrapping a comforting arm around his weeping sister.

Zuri stared at the different angles of the same event. "Where did you get these?"

"Archive footage." Rameen shrugged. "In this case, the sponsors kept it and let me have a copy. In other cases, surveillance footage survived."

Astonished, Zuri said, "You have

more?"

Instead of answering, Rameen replaced the images on the screens with other recordings. A store surveillance camera showing how a long-ago friend had tried to shoplift candy but Zuri stopped her. A school surveillance camera showed a girl immersed in a screen device walking onto a crosswalk and Zuri grabbing the girl's shoulder and hauling her back to the curb as a car sped past.

"You're not pulling these out of thin air," Zuri said. "You have them stored somewhere. How long have you had them? Why did you get them?"

Rameen turned to look at her. "Because you're my sister. When you disappeared ten years ago, this is how I found what was left of you. This is how I kept my sister in my life."

Zuri thought about the shift in the way her parents now perceived her. In Zuri's childhood, they'd ignored or misunderstood her. Since arriving in Middlesex Province, they'd acted like the parents she wished they had been. "You showed what you found of me to them. You showed them how they failed me."

He stood and turned off all the screens. "I like to think of it as inspiring them to do better, now that you're back in our lives."

"Who said I'm back in your life?" Zuri said. "That's not something you can tell me to do. It's my choice. Not yours."

Rameen's voice softened. "I was hoping you'd want to be my sister again."

"There's only one way that's going to happen," Zuri said. "Take me back to Vain-Glory."

CHAPTER 34

Following an afternoon flight and staying overnight on the mainland coast, Zuri arrived at VainGlory by drone taxi the next morning. She crossed the bullseye painted on the landing area as the drone took off, pleased with herself after giving Rameen and John the slip by waking up early and slipping away to catch the first taxi of the morning without them.

Smugness tugged at the corners of her mouth as she smiled.

I showed them!

Yesterday, Rameen had made Zuri reconsider how she lived her life with his sappy wish that she be part of their family again. He made her doubt her experience in VainGlory by showing her ridiculous footage of people calling for Zuri to be hung. Worst of all, Rameen claimed that Franklin

Buckingham—the biggest and brightest star of VainGlory—had manipulated her invitation to the city because her healthy heart proved to be the best genetic match to his failing one.

Shaking her head in disbelief, Zuri marveled at how she'd believed Rameen at the time, not realizing he probably fabricated everything he showed her. Now that she'd had time to think it over, Zuri doubted that anything Rameen had presented was real.

Last night, he'd said, "We can't afford to draw any kind of attention. Remember, the goal is to slip in, watch a fake version of you hang, and slip out."

Zuri liked the plan she'd thought of this morning much better. She'd go back to her home in the Platinum Tower, find a way to contact Donna, and describe how she'd been kidnapped by crazy family members. Once Zuri explained that her brother had forced her to remove her Personal Bubble, surely Donna would provide a new one.

Then life could go back to normal.

While she ambled down the walkway through the water garden toward the Carnival of Animals, the silence startled Zuri.

Where is everyone?

Zuri flexed her hand, where a small bandage covered a slight gash left after Rameen replaced her previous identity chip with a new one storing a copy of the identity and mosaic from a willing resident of Middlesex Province.

Just as Rameen promised, no streetlamp surveillance cameras noticed her presence. She walked through the water garden, invisible to all of VainGlory. Rameen had programmed this new chip so that it allowed her into the city without drawing any undue attention from its security system.

But Zuri had to move fast. Despite her pleas, he'd refused to remove the tracking device, which meant Rameen could find her. She assumed he and John would track her, and she didn't know how much time she had before they found her.

Zuri picked up her pace.

The water garden brought back uncomfortable memories of the mob that had chased her through it.

Zuri shook that memory away. No one had wanted to kill her. It had been a simple misunderstanding.

Once Zuri obtained a new bubble, she could set everything straight.

At the same time, she remembered something she'd seen this morning when she'd been in the air, approaching VainGlory.

But even now, Zuri couldn't be certain of what she'd seen when her airborne approach to the island gave a broad view of its shores. At first, Zuri saw the concentric rings of marinas around the island, all filled with yachts and other luxury boats. But then the Tall Ship building where Milan lived caught Zuri's attention because it appeared to shimmer.

Situated on its own concrete island like a lighthouse, Zuri had spotted the building only to lose sight of it as her drone taxi had banked, changing its angle toward Vain-Glory. Shaken, it had reminded her of art that tricked the eye: look at a drawing one way and you see a young woman. Look at the same drawing a different way and you see an elderly lady.

Except, in this case, the shape of the Tall Ship building didn't merely change.

The building appeared to vanish into thin air.

The same building where Milan lived.

An uncomfortable thought nagged at Zuri, and she decided to check up on her friend.

She remembered what Rameen had said last night.

Milan isn't real. She's a construct. A program designed to catch your attention and keep you occupied.

Just as she'd done last night, Zuri gave a bitter laugh. She spoke out loud, as if Rameen could hear her. "You're one to talk." She hesitated and spoke in a pointed voice. "Benjamin."

Rameen swore he'd checked the records

in VainGlory when he hacked in and found no record of anyone by the name of Milan existing. He said the Tall Ship where Milan lived was just an illusion.

What a bunch of nonsense.

A distant whirring caught her attention. Looking back, she saw a couple of drone taxis high in the air.

It had to be John and Rameen. They must have come awake earlier than she'd guessed and now wanted to force their plan on her.

They claimed Zuri's "hanging" was scheduled for late morning. That gave her plenty of time to check up on Milan. By the time Rameen and John could track Zuri, she'd be safe behind Milan's locked door.

Zuri veered off on another sidewalk leading away from the water garden. Wherever she walked, the city stood empty. Only rarely did she see anyone outside, and everyone in sight wore a maintenance uniform.

When Zuri had first arrived in Middlesex Province, she'd immediately noticed how many people spent time outside and that they all walked instead of using any kind of vehicle. Discovering she had to do the same, Zuri's muscles had ached at first but recently became accustomed to the amount of unwarranted exercise.

Now, she noticed an unexpected bounce in her step and steady breathing.

Previously, this kind of distance made her pant for air.

Rounding a corner, Zuri felt relief at the looming sight of the Tall Ship, apparently floating in the sea at the end of the street, looking forward to celebrating her return with Milan. Zuri felt even more excitement when she thought about how all of Vain-Glory would welcome her back.

Her step faltered when she looked up at the impinging Tall Ship only to see it shimmer.

It had to be a trick of the light. Maybe a cloud had passed overhead, and the returning sunlight had bounced off the building.

But the closer Zuri came toward the building, the more it looked like an image projected in the air. She saw the outer marinas through it—behind it. She rubbed her eyes, hoping that would help.

Impossible.

Zuri ran toward the Tall Ship. Where the street ended at the water's edge, a narrow pedestrian bridge connected to the Tall Ship. Zuri raced across it.

Gasping for breath when she reached the end of the bridge, Zuri choked on a foul stench.

She now stood on the concrete platform where she'd seen the Tall Ship stand. Still shimmering, the illusion of the building wavered all around her.

But an empty food delivery box crunched beneath her feet. Seagulls screamed and floated on extended wings beyond an incline ahead.

There was no tall ship, only a trash dump.

CHAPTER 35

Zuri felt dizzy as her entire world spun upside down and turned inside out. She backed up until her feet landed on the edge of the pedestrian bridge, where she clung to its railing to keep from collapsing into the field of garbage spread before her.

"Milan," she whispered, missing her VainGlory friend.

Is Rameen right? Was Milan nothing more than a program, like Benjamin?

Zuri's next thoughts sickened her. She'd confided in Milan. If Milan was a program, had that program been designed to extract information from Zuri? Private information that Zuri shared with few people? Was it now available to anyone who wanted it?

She remembered something else Rameen had told her last night.

Shepard Green was a construct, too. He's no more real than Milan.

Nausea crept along Zuri's throat. Still wobbly, she leaned over the bridge railing, thinking about every intimate moment she'd experienced with Shepard Green. Had that been elicited from her, too? Recorded? Made available to anyone who wanted to see it?

Shame filled every cell in Zuri's body.

How could I have been so stupid?

But then a new realization hit her.

Mae Lin was still in VainGlory. Were they doing the same to her as they'd done to Zuri?

Zuri shook her head. It couldn't be true. Even if what Rameen said about Buckingham was true—that he'd brought Zuri to VainGlory as an unsuspecting organ donor—that wouldn't apply to Mae Lin.

With a start, Zuri considered the fact that Mae Lin was a pretty girl. Someone like Buckingham and possibly his friends had other uses for pretty girls.

A new wave of shame filled Zuri as she realized she'd given no thought to Mae Lin since Shepard Green died.

How could I forget about Mae Lin? How could I forget about someone so important to me?

Zuri thought about the day she'd left her family, the way she'd pushed them away from her mind, determined to never think of them again.

Had it become a habit? Once she'd arrived in VainGlory, she'd forgotten about Aspire and everyone she knew there—with the exception of Mae Lin. But then Zuri had left VainGlory and forgotten Mae Lin.

Pushing away her shame and regret, Zuri turned her full attention to the task at hand. She had to find Mae Lin.

Last night, Rameen had shown her how to trigger a privacy wall and a tracer. Zuri pinched the skin covering her new identity chip, wincing at the pain. He told her she could use it to find anyone.

The light around Zuri turned pale gray, establishing the privacy wall.

A pinprick of red light hovered in front of Zuri, ready for a command.

"Mae Lin," Zuri told the light. "I want to find Mae Lin."

Zuri turned toward the island, scanning its crowded buildings. She noticed one that peeked above the others.

The Platinum Tower. Of course. That's where Mae Lin should be.

That's where Mae Lin *had* to be.

Before Zuri could run back across the bridge, the red light flickered and beeped.

A grid map of the city appeared in the air within Zuri's wall of privacy. The words "You are here" appeared clustered at the edge of the grid. The words "Mae Lin is here" materialized next to it, surrounded by three dots of bright yellow light.

"That can't be right," Zuri told the flashing red light. "You make it look like Mae Lin is standing here next to me. She's not."

The red light beeped louder.

The words "Mae Lin is here" were replaced with "Mae Lin is inside the dump."

* * *

Zuri rushed into the dump. She trudged through urban quicksand, ankle deep in putrid rubbish. Every uneven step threatened to turn her ankles, but Zuri pressed forward, climbing over hills of refuse. When she reached a crest and looked down below, her stomach turned.

Among the garbage and hidden by its mounds were dozens of scattered bodies, picked over by gulls.

It's my fault. Mae Lin is dead, and it's all my fault.

When Zuri tried to take another step, she lost her footing and slid next to one body far from the others. Scrambling to get back on her feet, Zuri froze when she recognized the woman's face.

Karen.

Her rival's clothes had been ripped apart and left hanging like an afterthought on her lifeless form.

Despite the strange hue of the woman's

skin, Zuri touched her wrist to search for a pulse. When she felt the cold, stiff limb, Zuri dropped it with a cry.

The stench rising from Karen's body made Zuri gag. She wanted to run and get away from the horror around her.

But failing Mae Lin in life was no excuse for failing her in death. Zuri couldn't leave until she found Mae Lin.

Gathering all her strength, Zuri ignored the reek of the dead mixed with trash and kept searching until what she found made her heart drop. The sight of her friend's battered and bloody face made Zuri catch her breath, along with the recognition that the clothing she wore had been ripped.

Sinking next to her, Zuri's hand trembled as she placed her bare fingers against Mae Lin's neck.

Although faint and cool to the touch, Mae Lin's neck pulsed against Zuri's fingers.

"Mae Lin!" Zuri cried out in joyful relief. She took her friend's hand and squeezed it. "Mae Lin, I'm here. You're safe."

The blades of two drone taxis chopped the air as they descended toward the marina and the dump that Zuri once believed to be the Tall Ship building.

Looking up, Zuri said, "It's Rameen and John. They'll help us get out of here."

A whistling sound pierced the air above.

Zuri looked up to see missiles strike the

drone taxis, which exploded and fell into the water below.

CHAPTER 36

Zuri screamed.

Mae Lin's eyes opened. "Zuri?"

Zuri tried to pick Mae Lin up in her arms but didn't have the strength to lift her. Instead, she dragged her friend up the hill of refuse. "We have to find a place to hide."

When they ascended to the peak of the dump, Zuri heard distant cheers. Looking up, she saw smoke rise from a streetlamp, still aimed at where the drone taxis had been in the sky.

Rameen and John are dead. The city killed them.

Grief weighed heavy, but Zuri pushed it aside. Taking the time for grief right now would get Zuri and Mae Lin killed, too. Zuri could cry later.

"Get up," Zuri said to a barely-conscious Mae Lin. "We can hide in plain sight at my apartment. That should give us time to figure out how to get out of here."

Mae Lin struggled to her feet and clung to Zuri as they walked.

But when they reached the street, all of the streetlamps turned to face them.

"We should be invisible," Zuri whispered.

She then realized Mae Lin still had her identity chip, connecting her to the entire city. Their only chance of escaping meant taking that chip out of Mae Lin's hand. But Zuri had nothing capable of getting the job done.

Keeping hold of Mae Lin, Zuri backed both of them up until she felt the uneven ground of the dump beneath her feet. Zuri cast her gaze across it until she spotted something bright and sharp. She dragged Mae Lin with her, picked up a rusty, broken steak knife, and dug into the flesh of Mae Lin's hand until the chip fell out.

Mae Lin screamed in dismay.

The distant streetlamps stared at them.

Using one hand to keep a tight grip on Mae Lin, Zuri reached down with the other to pick up the bloody chip and hurled it toward the bridge. The chip sparkled in the sunlight as it flew over the railing and into the waters of the marina below.

In unison, the streetlamps followed the flight of the chip and focused their attention on where it splashed into the water.

Mae Lin stared in horror at her hand. "What have you done? Where is my mosaic?"

"Let's go get it," Zuri said, knowing she had to lie. Keeping her hold on Mae Lin, Zuri said, "This way." She headed away from where she'd thrown Mae Lin's chip. The sidewalk appeared to circle around the dump, and Zuri knew there were boats docked on the other side. She remembered how Donna told her that VainGlorians kept their keys in the ignition. Zuri and Mae Lin could steal a boat and get back to the mainland.

But Mae Lin dug her heels in, refusing to leave. "That's the wrong way. Why won't you let me get my mosaic back?"

The women struggled but managed to do little more than stay in place. Only the cries from the city made them stop.

Looking down the length of the street ahead, Zuri saw a mob round a corner. She remembered what Rameen had told her about the city wanting to hang her today. "It's too late. They found us."

"Where is my mosaic?" Mae Lin shrieked.

Desperate to make her friend understand that their lives depended on escaping the crowd, Zuri pointed toward the water. "I threw it away. It's the only way we can get out of here!"

Hysterical, Mae Lin stumbled toward

the water. "I have to get it back! It's my life!"

In that moment, Zuri saw herself in Mae Lin.

My mosaic is my life.

Zuri lunged toward Mae Lin, wrapping her arms around her friend's waist.

Zuri remembered what John had told her.

You're not made up of things.

"You're not made up of things," Zuri told Mae Lin. "Your true mosaic is who you are. Not what you buy. Not the things you like. Not the things you say. Your true mosaic is what you do. How you act in the world. How you treat other people."

Mae Lin kicked Zuri away and scrambled toward the water. "Murderer! You killed Shepard Green. I won't let you murder me, too."

Zuri tackled Mae Lin before she could tumble into the water below. Holding her friend's arms behind her back, Zuri pinned her to the ground.

Mae Lin screamed for help.

Wincing in pain from Mae Lin's well-placed kick, Zuri saw the distant mob creep closer, their angry cries growing louder. The lamps in the streetlights turned on, placing bright yellow spotlights on the two women.

Zuri stood.

Weak and fatigued, Mae Lin hauled herself onto her feet and stumbled toward the crowd, waving her arms to get their attention.

I did this. Mae Lin said we should take our profit and stay in Aspire. I'm the one who brought Mae Lin to VainGlory. Everything that happened to her is my fault.

In desperation, and with all her strength, Zuri tripped Mae Lin, who tumbled back to the ground.

Mae Lin screamed in pain. "You broke my ankle!"

I doubt it.

"Stay put," Zuri said. "I'm coming back for you."

Satisfied that Mae Lin couldn't run away, Zuri sprinted around the dump, soon circling behind it. Faced with seemingly acres of boats docked on the other side, Zuri stopped for a second, then ran down the first walkway between the rows of boats until she found one with keys in the ignition. She jumped onboard the empty boat. Starting it up with a roar, she backed it out of the slip to the best of her ability, scraping against the end of another boat protruding from its own slip.

Zuri accelerated in fits and starts as she navigated the boat alongside the same circular path she'd just run. Pulling up next to Mae Lin's huddled figure, Zuri let the boat idle. She unfurled a rope ladder over the side, climbed down it, and hurried back onto shore.

The mob now ran toward them, gaining ground.

"Come on," Zuri said. "Let's find your mosaic."

Mae Lin brightened at the mention of her mosaic.

Zuri hauled Mae Lin onto her feet and dragged her toward the boat. Mae Lin leaned on Zuri, hobbling on one leg as they waded into the water. Zuri climbed the rope ladder, pulling Mae Lin up behind her.

Ignoring the encroaching mob, Zuri heard their splashes as they entered the water from the opposite shore. Shouting, angry people surged toward the boat.

After settling Mae Lin down on the deck, Zuri whipped the boat down the waterway, knocking away a stranger who tried to grab the ladder that Zuri had forgotten to pull back up.

As the boat escaped the outreaching hands of the people behind it, Mae Lin cried out in horror. "My mosaic! We have to find my mosaic!" She crawled to the railing and hauled herself up against it. Weeping, Mae Lin stretched her arms toward the angry mob behind them. "Fame is the name of the game," she called out in wretched desperation.

Zuri remembered what Mae Lin had said about Zuri's insistence on striving for fame on the day of their first success in VainGlory.

Does that matter anymore?

The boat sped from one marina through another. Angry sirens echoed among the skyscrapers. The streetlamps scattered throughout the city cast thick searchlight beams that crossed in reckless abandon, searching in desperation for what the city's security system could no longer detect.

Zuri ignored the throbbing pain in her stomach from where her friend had kicked her.

"I'm sorry I forgot you," Zuri said before she realized the roar of the boat's engine would make it impossible for Mae Lin to hear her words. Zuri glanced back to see Mae Lin sink her head into her hands and sob.

Zuri focused on navigating the narrow and maze-like lanes of the marina and the tiny resident islands surrounding it.

"We'll be home soon," Zuri shouted.

"Home," Mae Lin moaned. She struggled to her knees and reached weakly over the rail toward a nearby boardwalk.

Something sparkled in one of the wandering searchlights far beyond it, capturing Zuri's attention.

She recognized a herd of crystal deer sauntering through the Carnival of Animals park. The searchlight penetrated the creatures, casting huge prisms of light throughout the park and high into the air and across the cityscape, like a benediction of rainbows.

The beauty of the light tugged at Zuri, making her remember how wonderful she'd felt in VainGlory. How everything she'd dreamed of during the past ten years had finally come true. How all her hard work had finally paid off. How she'd earned and deserved all the success and attention and wealth.

"Home," Mae Lin shouted above the noisy boat. She looked at Zuri with tears streaking her face. "I want to go home!"

Faint music wafted through the city, singing like mythological sirens luring sailors into the depths of the sea.

Rameen had been right about Milan and Shepard Green. They weren't real. Zuri remembered the mob that had chased her through the city and how she'd hidden inside a fountain to escape them. She thought about Karen's dead body and how Mae Lin had been left for dead.

And yet, the city's beautiful song and majestic sights wrapped around her with such grandeur that she let those thoughts drift away like an outgoing tide.

The boat took a sharp turn and hugged the boardwalk as it wrapped around the harbor, heading back toward the bullseye where Zuri had first landed in VainGlory.

Now, the hundreds of vibrant fountains in the water park came into view, streams of water dancing to the rhythm of the city's serenade.

Zuri stared at the fountains, torn between the wonder of their beauty and her memory of hiding inside one.

But all the fountains stopped working, and their streams fell nosily. Moments later, pale green fog emerged from the fountains instead of water, creating a blanket of air that spread into the marina.

Zuri gave into her impulse to turn her head and sniff at an approaching arm of the green fog. She let the heady scent of jasmine wrap around her.

Zuri eased her foot off of the accelerator, and the boat slowed to drift in the marina.

Mae Lin shouted, "Come with me!" She made a feeble attempt to stand, but her legs betrayed her and buckled. She collapsed on deck.

Zuri wanted to shake some sense into her friend but couldn't force herself to move. Why couldn't she? She wanted to help Mae Lin.

But I don't want to help Mae Lin. I want to go with her.

It would be so easy to dive into the water, so warm and pleasant. It wouldn't take long to swim through the harbor and climb up on shore. The fountains would greet them, along with the animated flowers and crystal animals. Everything would be fine.

Zuri wanted her life to go back to the way it used to be.

Her life was perfect in VainGlory. She needed it to be perfect again.

Mae Lin managed to pull her body to lean against the rail and balanced on one leg. She looked ready to jump into the water before the distance between the boat and the shore became too great.

Zuri wanted to dive into the warmth of the sea. She wanted to ignore everything she'd seen and experienced during her last few days in VainGlory.

She wanted to pretend nothing was wrong. She didn't care if the city might kill her or Mae Lin. At least, they'd die in a place where they'd been deliriously happy.

A mechanical voice blared like a loudspeaker. "Criminal offense!"

The searchlights turned and swept toward Zuri's stolen boat.

"I didn't mean to steal anything," Zuri shouted over the racket of the idling engine. "I'm not leaving. I want to stay!"

But the searchlights swept over Zuri and closer to where the marina opened into the sea. The beams of light cut through the water, clear and clean.

The lights landed on two men swimming in from the sea and toward Zuri.

She recognized them at once. Zuri waved at them. "Rameen! John! You're alive!"

The mechanical voice blasted again. "Criminal offense. Charged with criminal trespass. Found guilty. Death sentence to be executed immediately."

Death sentence?

The water between the boat and the swimming men churned and bubbled. In dismay, Zuri ran to the rail and looked down into the clear water to see a large cage at the bottom of its depths. The cage door raised, and a shark swam out of it.

As if her life were flashing before her eyes, Zuri remembered the beauty of Vain-Glory and everything she'd experienced inside its limits. She still wanted to go back.

Instead, she raced to the wheel and slammed on the accelerator. Before the shark could surface, Zuri reached the swimming men, guiding the boat so that the rope ladder she'd forgotten to pull up now faced them. "Hurry!" she shouted. "There's a shark!"

Their faces drawn with exhaustion, Rameen and John plowed through the water.

Zuri rifled through the boat, looking for a gun or harpoon or some other kind of weapon. Her only luck came when she found a flare gun. She hurried to the rail, searching for the shark.

Rameen reached the rope ladder first, grunting as he hauled himself up and flung his body on board. Immediately, he turned, ready to help John.

The water bubbled and churned around the boat, making it difficult for Zuri to see below the surface. "John!" she shouted. "Hurry!"

Head down, John slapped his arms through the water, drawing near.

Zuri saw something large and dark beneath him. She took aim with the flare gun, hands trembling.

As John reached toward the ladder, the shark's jaws broke through the surface of the water, aiming toward his legs.

Screaming in terror, Zuri fired at the animal's open mouth, where the flare exploded moments later.

Rameen grabbed John's outreached hand and helped him up on board.

John winced. "It got me."

Horrified, Zuri watched blood bloom beneath a tear in John's pant leg.

Rameen peeled off his soaked shirt and wrapped it tightly about John's injured leg. "I've got this," he told Zuri. "Get us out of here."

Looking back, Zuri saw Mae Lin crumpled on the deck. Wondering if she'd died, Zuri sighed in relief at the sight of the fall and rise of her friend's chest.

Taking the wheel again, Zuri gunned the boat through the last stretch of the marina and into the open sea. The boat escaped the perfume of the city. The scent of brine filled Zuri's nose like smelling salts, shocking her back to her senses.

She glanced back at VainGlory as it shrank in the distance, framed by walls of water kicked up by the speeding boat. The city continued to sing, refusing to give up on the women. The pale green fog hung over it in low-lying clouds. The bright white search beams now cut through that fog, illuminating the magnificent skyline like clusters of beckoning phantoms.

Zuri focused on the distant shore of the mainland ahead, trying to ignore the raw and ravenous craving for VainGlory and hoped for a day when she would be free of it.

Author's Note

Although this is a work of fiction, it is based on fact.

While researching this novel, I took online courses, read nonfiction books, re-read classic novels, revisited film footage I'd taken at museum exhibits, and watched documentaries. I highly recommend the following sources:

- *The Shallows: What the Internet is Doing to Our Brains* by Nicholas Carr. This book was a Finalist for the Pulitzer Prize.
- *The Social Dilemma*. This NetFlix documentary is about the way companies use social media and how their decisions and actions impact us without our knowledge.

Some of the fashions in this book were inspired by real clothing featured in a past exhibit at the Museum of Fine Arts, Boston. The bubble dress (worn by Zuri and designed by Mae Lin) was inspired by the CuteCircuit's MFA Dress (2016) by Francesca Rosella and Ryan Genz. The red coat (worn by Karen) with a life of its own was inspired by the Possessed Dress (2015) by Hussein Chalayan. The porcupine dress (worn by Karen) was inspired by the Incertitudes Shirt and Shorts (2013) by Ying Gao.

THE MOSAIC WOMAN

ABOUT THE AUTHOR

Resa Nelson began her writing journey as a short story writer, selling over 20 stories to magazines and anthologies.

She is a longtime member of Science Fiction Writers of America and a graduate of the Clarion Science Fiction Writers Workshop. She currently has more than 20 novels published.

THE MOSAIC WOMAN

Other Novels by Resa Nelson

All of Us Were Sophie

Our Lady of the Absolute

The Dragonslayer series:

The Dragonslayer's Sword
The Iron Maiden
The Stone of Darkness
The Dragon's Egg

The Dragonfly series:

Dragonfly
Dragonfly in the Land of Ice
Dragonfly in the Land of Swamp Dragons
Dragonfly in the Land of Sleeping Giants

The Dragon Gods series:

Gate of Air
Gate of Earth
Gate of Fire
Gate of Water

(continued on next page)

The Dragon Seed series:

Berserk
The Dragonslayer's Heart
The Dragonslayer's Curse
The Dragonslayer's Fate

Demon Queller books:

The Yellow Dragon

The Dragon Bells

To learn more about Resa Nelson's books, visit resanelson.com or her author's page on Amazon.com.

THE MOSAIC WOMAN

CPSIA information can be obtained
at www.ICGtesting.com
Printed in the USA
BVHW011330030622
638826BV00015B/48

9 798734 523445